The Hounds of Hades

The Hounds of Hades

JOYCE STRANGER

Michael Joseph
London

First published in Great Britain by
Michael Joseph Ltd
44 Bedford Square
London WC1B 3DU
1985

British Library Cataloguing in Publication Data

Stranger, Joyce
The hounds of Hades.
I. Title
823'.914[F]   PR6069.T68
ISBN 0 7181 2592 4

Typeset by Action Typesetting, Gloucester
Printed in Great Britain by Hollen Street Press, Slough
and bound by Hunter & Foulis Ltd, Edinburgh

Dedicated to Liz Moores
with the greatest gratitude.
She makes my books possible by doing all the
household chores I don't have time for, and has
done for the past eight years.

PART I   The Inheritance

CHAPTER 1

Great Uncle Joel died just in time to save me from going mad.

Great Uncle Joel the mystery man. The man who lived alone; the man who lived for horses. The man who never married; the man who hated people. The man who refused to see visitors; the man who did not acknowledge his relations. He would have nothing to do with his sisters. The man who had walked out on his family; who disappeared for over twenty years and then reappeared as a very rich man.

The man who bred the best racehorses in the country, starting from nothing, coming from no-where.

The man who, astoundingly, left everything he owned to me, his great nephew, Joel. We had never met.

I was twenty-four when Great Uncle Joel died. I was the squarest peg in the roundest hole that anyone ever found for a man. I had been like that all my life. Born in the city, enclosed by the city, imprisoned by the city, and hating the city.

I am the youngest and there are four of us. My sister adores her prison; adores the trim little nest she has built for herself; adores the trappings that surround her. She loves dressing her elegant body and making up her pretty little face; there are mirrors in every room in the house, so that she can admire her reflection. Yet, oddly, she revels in the daily chores associated with the baby. He's quite a nice baby as babies go, but she thinks, dreams and talks of nothing but her tiny son. I visit her and we sit in polite emptiness, saying words that have no meaning, to me at least.

She loves giving little dinner parties for her unmarried friends to which she can invite her oh-so-eligible brother. I am left alone while she and her husband wash the dishes and make the coffee, taking so long over the simple tasks. Alone with Susan or Debbie or Marina or Elizabeth; always such pretty girls, with lovely faces and happy voices, with everything a pretty girl should have except the spark that brings me to life.

My mother does the same thing. I am sure that she and my sister conspire together, determined to trap me in a feminine snare, to clip my wings for ever. Mother even laughs gently and calls me her untamed hawk. I swallow my retort for the sake of family peace, and resolve to leave it even longer before I visit again. I have been there once, in the marriage trap. Not yet, not again, perhaps not ever.

My brothers are identical twins; they never had time for anyone but themselves, and though they are both married, they live near one another. Their wives do not seem to mind that their lifetime commitment to each other goes on; they spend more time together than with their partners, eternally bound in a way that the rest of us find difficult to understand. I sometimes wonder if the children actually know which one is their father; both are so alike, both spend so much time together. The children, fortunately, are not in the least alike; the boys resemble their mothers. Except for Darren, who looks very like me and has inherited my passion for horses.

It is odd that passions are born in families; we are as

4

much victims of our inheritance as are dogs, showing their breeding, or racehorses, that show theirs and run true to form.

Great Uncle Joel's grandfather bred horses, Shire horses. There is a portrait of the most famous of his champions hanging over my dining-room fireplace in the farmhouse that Great Uncle Joel lived in. Maybe his grandfather's ancestors were also horse breeders and cattle breeders. They have handed down his genes to me and I am driven by that inheritance. Nothing can alter that. We are as we are born, and Great Uncle Joel was that too; but he was less lucky than any of us. He had to make his own luck, and he made mine too.

Nobody understood what I wanted, what I needed; or that I was in prison, in the terrible city, that dictated how I lived. Speed limits and walk here and don't walk on the grass; keep left and no entry. Even now the money I work for is only partly mine; so much of it belongs to the State. I am a very rich man now. I pay enormous taxes as a penalty – rich men are frowned upon. Never mind that the money is gained by hard work, by unremitting work, twenty-four hours a day at times. We don't live in a State-run society, so they say. Oh, but we do, we do. Those around me don't even know they are imprisoned by convention, by laws, by society. Are patterned by society to regard rich men and great rewards as unacceptable.

I employ twenty hands. Without me they might well have no work. Does that make me unacceptable? I was born a rebel, like Great Uncle Joel. I suppose it does make me unacceptable to many. I find the world I live in very difficult to understand. I am safest with my horses. They ask nothing of me except that I care for them and feed them, and they reward me with affection.

I don't want to break laws, or even break the ten commandments. Though I did find it hard not to covet. I couldn't have what I coveted, not until Great Uncle Joel died and handed me heaven.

Heaven, as always, had its serpent hidden. When I inherited his home, went to work with his horses, and began to fulfill every need I ever had, I found that Great Uncle Joel's business was apparently based on a fraud; and I don't know what to do.

I don't know what he did. All his life he kept diaries; detailed accounts of the stud; one for each year since 1930. They make fascinating reading. I am going through them, day by day, learning a great deal about horses.

The day books are full of horse lore. He left a note saying I must read them as they will help me with the daily running of the business. I don't know if he realised they revealed so much of his thoughts, and of his life, or of his frequent remorse for that unknown crime that I can't even identify.

He wrote, just before he died: 'I am not sorry; yet daily I feel remorse, as I have the money under false pretences. I am haunted by regret. I do not know how to repay. The Hounds bay for ever.'

I am slowly reading through, trying to re-create his life, trying to find out what crime he committed; it must be somewhere in these pages. I can't benefit from a fraud. But oh, Great Uncle Joel, if the truth is unbearable, what shall I do? Sell everything and return the money to the rightful owner?

What is his secret? I search and search and I still can't find an answer. I am going to write it all down, as I read it, year by year, from the beginning. Perhaps the truth will appear. I owe you so much; I have inherited your fortune. Your horses are now my horses and I could not bear to part with them. But I can't inherit your guilt; I could not live with that.

His grooms remember him as a just man, but a man who had little to say to them. He would not stand for any abuse of his horses; the horses came first, last and all the time. Nothing else mattered to him. He looked like me – we have the same eyes, dark brown, long catlike eyes; the same hair, thick and curly, and blond. The same shaped mouth. He, like me, was a big man, tall and well built; and perhaps he, as I have, had within him a well of damped-down violence, an impatience, an anger, a ferocity that rarely appeared on the surface. He is revealed, in his photographs, taken always with a horse, as a stern man, unsmiling. He did not seem to know laughter. I can laugh at my foals' and my mares' gentle absurdities; perhaps Great Uncle Joel laughed too when he was alone. It is plain from what I have read so far that he trusted no one.

Perhaps all that I dare do is write it down, to be published long after I too am dead. Can you be sent to prison for another man's crime?

Great Uncle Joel, you have given me the life I love; but sometimes I wonder if the price you exacted from me is not too high. Yet how can I go back to the stifling city streets, join the daily rush hour, walk with the push and thrust of bodies close to me all day, when I have the wide hills here in the distance, and the blue sky, and the paddocks and the pastures and the cattle I inherited and the life that my parents denied me because they never understood my needs?

I was born a misfit and you freed me. Did you know that I inherited your passion? Did you watch me, perhaps using those detectives whose bills figure mysteriously in your accounts, knowing that whenever I could I left the city and walked on the hills and savoured every mare and every foal I met, talking to them over gates, longing to own those fantastic creatures that race on the downs, and fly against the wind and are worth more than diamonds or gold to those of us that share the passion?

Where does it come from, this urgent need, this obsession? Perhaps, as I read, I shall find out.

I doubt if I will ever marry again. That was brief madness. We were both far too young. There was nothing behind the façade. She was beautiful and foolish and her silliness irked me daily. I am glad she is gone. I could never have told her the truth.

I am going to write this story as if it were a novel, a fiction, and remove it from reality, by pretence. Perhaps if I do so I will work out what to do for the best; I suspect I will live for ever with my knowledge and leave this manuscript as part of his inheritance to my own heir.

Great Uncle Joel, you broke the law. Or did you? Perhaps it was only a commandment that you broke and men do that daily without being discovered; not one of the major sins, like murder; a little sin, if there is such a thing as a little sin. You prospered through your misdeed. You gave me a future. I can't betray you, but I must write down what I know, or I cannot live with myself.

You say you shouldn't have done it. But I am so glad you did. Does that make me an accessory?

This is your story. I am going to write it down and I am going to see if I can get it published. Maybe then someone, reading it, will divine the truth and write to me and tell me what I ought to do.

Do you rest in peace, Uncle Joel? Or is your ghost haunting me, driving me to write the story, keeping me awake at night, because I cannot sleep for thinking of it?

Then dawn comes, and I go to see my mares, and

talk to my grooms. I remember the city and know that, almost certainly, I will live as you did, telling no one and hoping that those who read my book, which will be published under an assumed name to hide my identity, will never guess the truth or realise that it is the description of your misdeed. I will, perhaps, have quieted my own conscience.

Maybe when this is published we will both sleep peacefully. Rest in peace, Great Uncle Joel. I won't betray you. If I did I would betray myself, and sentence myself to a living death, away from the life I love, as it would all go. Wouldn't it?

You speak of the Hounds of Hades baying at your heels. They bay at mine now, driving me down a long road that leads to a living hell, as I will inherit your guilt.

Great Uncle Joel, what *did* you do?

CHAPTER 2

Each large book was dated meticulously. Great Uncle Joel had obviously been taught by his grandfather; taught how to keep those massive accounts of every mare; of every mating; of every foaling, and every foal. So he documented his own life, the small clues to his daily doings interspersed amongst the records of horses.

Later, when he had become well known, each horse had its own separate record book, which started with a photograph of the animal, then its pedigree, its birth, its growth, its fate, as to whether kept for breeding or sold; and if it was sold, he followed a horse's racing history all through its life.

He had obviously been a solitary man.

The early diaries did refer to his feelings and to his early life; he felt betrayed by his own parents, and he also felt an implacable hatred of them that hardened with the years. He had a fierce belief in destiny; he was sure he was destined to live and work with horses.

Oddly, too, he was certain that destiny guided him from the time of my birth. I looked up that year out of curiosity and was startled to find another record book, a different colour from the rest, with my name on it in gold letters. Joel David Tate. Born 27th May 1954. He noted that he had seen in the columns of the *Daily Telegraph* the details of the birth of a son, Joel David, to Jonathan and Sheila Tate.

He wrote that maybe here, with such a name, would be another chip off the old block, a man worthy of his great-great-grandfather.

It is then that the bills from the detective agency started. They were in a plastic envelope which was taped into the front of the book. I was startled, and a little disturbed to think that someone had been watching me all those years, and I hadn't known.

He made a note that this indeed was his own great nephew. The agency had investigated my parents, and discovered their parentage; and a family research organisation had traced all Great Uncle Joel's relatives; there were records of his sisters' marriages, and of their sons' births; and of their sons' sons. He had watched us all, from a distance. He had never seen or met any of us. None of my uncles or cousins had the slightest interest in horses.

After the confirmation that I am indeed his great nephew there is an annual record; to ensure that I was healthy and, later, when I escaped from home on any occasion I could, and rode any horse I could borrow, the satisfaction grows. He knew that I haunted our local stables, borrowed horses from my friends, worked in the stables at weekends, asking only for riding lessons in return.

He knew when I started school and the name of the school; he knew when I changed schools; he knew when I left school. The knowledge was necessarily sketchy; he had not made in-depth investigations for which I was grateful. It was strange to think that for all those years eyes had been watching me grow up, eyes that I never knew existed.

He guessed at my frustration when I was forced into the advertising agency. He knew the futility of a life spent selling products that nobody wanted to people who couldn't afford them.

11

He recorded my marriage, and his satisfaction when it ended. Ronna fitted into my advertising life; she didn't fit anywhere else. I couldn't ever satisfy her insatiable need for the good things of this life: the furs and the jewels and the expensive clothes; the smart furniture that emulated the Jones'; the cocktail parties and the nights out; and the fringe of a scene that I never wanted to share – the frantic, frenetic, unsatisfying and horrifying pop scene.

I escaped more and more often, at weekends, to the countryside, for long solitary walks on the hills, to yearning talks with any horse who stuck his wise head over a gate and told me that the things Ronna valued and the aims she had made for me were senseless. I always ended at some riding stables, hiring a horse for the afternoon, riding out into duneland or downland, moorland or mountainland; forgetting in the ecstasy of being once more with a horse, the misery that dogged my marriage.

Riding helped me to forget, briefly, the evenings when I went home to an empty house, and went out for an indifferent meal as there was nothing there to cook. To forget the lonely weekends when Ronna was away; the emptiness of a home that was no home at all; that, when she was there, was filled with noise and people and brittle hateful laughter. I was their butt, their fool; I never saw their jokes or understood their innuendoes.

I walked out of that marriage only a year later, at a party, one hectic evening when Ronna vanished with the drummer from a famous pop group and didn't return for four days. When she returned I had gone, taking only the few things I valued, among them the little statuette of a horse that I had bought and paid a fortune for; a fortune that Ronna had expected would buy her a diamond bracelet she had seen at Cartier's.

12

She was very beautiful; very sweet when she had her own way; and in my eyes she betrayed me, over and over, with modern ways and modern morals that I didn't share. I was born monogamous; one man, one woman. I wanted children with security in their lives. I had married in haste and repented at leisure. The old saws may be corny but they often hide a germ of truth. Luckily there were no children and I could escape from the trap.

It is a beautiful little statuette; it is on my desk now. The mare is perfect, her lovely head held on a proudly arched neck, her legs flying, her tail flying behind her, an ecstasy of movement. It is an investor's piece by a famous sculptor, but that is not why I bought it. I bought it because I was enthralled; it embodied, for me, everything I longed for and would never have. It was symbol of a future that could never be mine, a symbol of freedom from city ways and city streets. I coveted it as Ronna coveted jewellery.

I would have stolen for it and could understand men who have killed for a much-desired object. I lusted for it. I have not wanted anything else quite so badly in my life; not until the astonishing day I discovered I had inherited all I ever wanted and become rich beyond my dreams; not in money, but in a way of life that meant more to me than life itself. Ronna never forgave me for buying the little mare. Nothing could ever equal the wild excitement of that day.

I was able, unexpectedly, to buy the mare because I had had a big win on Ernie; the money was mine, from a gamble; not earned, and not for Ronna, and I wanted to invest it in something I would cherish; not in jewels for my fickle wife. And not in stocks and shares; not to lie in a bank account, earning interest, but giving me no pleasure. I was young with the future ahead and I had strength and my brains and

13

could earn more money; I could never find anything so beautiful as the little mare. It gave me endless pleasure just to sit and look at her, to savour her, to admire her lines, her shape, the lustre of the bronze from which she was made.

She is on my desk as I write; the desk that belonged to Great Uncle Joel, and I know he would have loved her as I love her.

Great Uncle Joel's record book brought back those days with Ronna. The passion, and the bitterness, and the grief for a broken dream. I had thought that I had forgotten them, but the hurt is just as fresh, all these years later. I had loved a woman who only existed in my imagination, and marriage had revealed the horrid reality. Yet somehow that imaginary woman still held me in thrall. I had dreamed of Elaine, and married Circe. Maybe that has happened all through history.

I leafed through his record book; my life was documented uncannily; he had explained that in a letter that came to me when he died:

To the Great Nephew I have never met,
I hope you will forgive me for keeping you under surveillance. You will understand if you accept your legacy, and read my records, why I have never wished to meet any of my family again. I do not wish to meet you, lest I am disappointed. I have dreamed too long of you as my successor; have watched a boy grow up, living as I might have lived, with parents who approve of him. I grieved over your foolish marriage as they must have grieved. I have had full reports on you. Try to think of me not as a man who watched over you, not as a spy, but as a second father. I do not regret never having had a wife; I bitterly regret that I never had a son. I know you love horses, although whether

14

you share my passion I cannot yet tell. You have never been given the chance to prove yourself. I prefer not to know whether you will take the opportunity I offer, or whether you will betray me, as my father betrayed me, and sell your inheritance as he sold mine. I offer you my idea of heaven because I feel it is your heaven; whether it is or not is entirely up to you. I am not going to plead, nor to influence you.

My only hope as I grow old, and perhaps senile, is that horses and the life I know will be part of me forever; if not, all I ask is for dreamless peace. I cannot bear the thought of leaving my horses among strangers who will not care for them as I have cared for them. I hope, with all my heart, that I have not judged you wrongly and that you will follow the path I have made for you.

If you sell, you will have the money that your wife has always coveted; she may return to you, if you so wish.

If you refuse to carry on where I leave off, you are not the man I thought you, and I will have no regrets because you would not honour your commitments or work for your horses, to keep them as I kept them.

I can only ask that whatever fates control our idiot lives will inspire you to accept your destiny because I would like to rest knowing my work was not wasted and went on through yet another Joel, a chip off the old block, a worthy great-great-grandson for the only person in my life for whom I ever cared, my grandfather, Joel Martin.

I do not believe in God, or in an after-life, so can only wish you well, provided you follow me here, in the only place where I have known happiness. If not, then I cannot find it in my heart to wish you any future at all.

My family made me what I am. I hope that yours have done better for you; I am offering you a chance, should you need it, to escape from your square hole, which I believe you hate, to a niche that fits you perfectly.

In all sincerity,
Your Great Uncle Joel

The letter is in front of me now; written in black ink, in heavy writing, the loops strangely elongated and angular, the words almost driven into the thick paper. His power comes to me through that letter, and everything his men say, remembering him, confirms that impression. A fair man, a just man, a stern man, a man with a raging fury in him if a horse was neglected or harmed. A big man, big as I am, with a mass of white hair and a thick flowing beard. My hair is blond as his was.

'I always felt he looked like God,' Johnnie, the youngest stable lad said once. 'He was terrifying.'

Johnnie looked at me anxiously. He was a tiny boy, looking far younger than his seventeen years, always worried in case he offended. I laughed, and he smiled at me and went off hastily, back to his cherished horse. Johnnie had only one fault: he lived in the stable with his mare and it was hard to make him leave her. He had come from a children's home where his mother had dumped him when he was a year old. Nobody had ever had time to love Johnnie and all the pent-up devotion of his empty years was given to his mare. How well Great Uncle Joel must have understood him.

I spent the first year of my new life at the stud farm reading those record books, filling in the details, gaining knowledge of the life of my great uncle; and of the long years that had preceded his buying of the farm.

It was an astonishing story.

PART II   Great Uncle Joel's Story

CHAPTER 3

Ellen Martin married late. At thirty, she had expected to remain unwed for the rest of her life. She was a plain woman, knowing little of feminine wiles. James David, a friend of her father, came visiting. He was newly widowed and when a decent time had elapsed James David asked Ellen to marry him. He needed a housekeeper more than a wife. He needed a woman to wash his clothes and prepare his meals. Ellen, only too grateful to be freed from the tyranny of living with her father, whom she thought uncouth, and freed of the constant hated chores that went with the farm, walked gratefully to the altar.

She made a good wife. She bore James four daughters, all biddable girls. She, deprived of social graces, delighted in teaching them pretty manners and pretty ways. They sang and recited and learned the piano and ballroom dancing. They knitted and sewed and became skilled cooks. Ellen was determined her daughters should wed before they were twenty.

She named them prettily: Helene, Suzanne, Diane and Louise. It was the only unexpected thing she ever did; such names as Gladys and Edith and Hilda were in vogue. There was one year's difference between each child. Helene, born in 1900, was the eldest, followed by Suzanne, born in 1901, Diane, born in 1902, and Louise, the baby, born in 1903.

By the time all four girls were born James had risen

from his place at the bank counter to the post of manager of one of the smaller banks in a small country town. Ellen was able to employ a housemaid and a parlour maid to help her, and a mother's help, known to everyone as Misnid. It did not occur to the little girls that these were two separate words.

By early 1903 the family was complete; there were to be no more children. Ellen employed herself usefully with various committees and was a well-respected member of the Church.

Life was settled and placid. James enjoyed his place in the town's society; he played bridge twice every week with the rector and two local solicitors. His day was ordered: he rose at seven-thirty each morning, with time for a leisurely breakfast of bacon and eggs, or perhaps a piece of haddock, followed by toast and marmalade. The girls ate with Misnid in a little morning room off the hall and only appeared to kiss their father goodbye before he took up his rolled umbrella and set off for the Bank. The Bank was a place regarded with awe, where Father wielded great power.

There was considerable dismay on the part of both Ellen and her husband when, late in 1908, she found herself pregnant again. Ellen was nearly forty years old; birth at that age was even more likely to be fraught with hazard than at a younger age. A baby would not fit into her way of life at all, but she resigned herself, as there was nothing else she could do.

The baby was born on a blustery night in late May 1909. To James's pleasure and his wife's dismay the child was a boy. They christened him Peter Joel, after Ellen's father. The old man, grinning down at his grandson at the ceremony, commented that here indeed at last was a lusty young cockerel and high

20

time too. He didn't want to see nothing but girls as his descendants. The remark did not endear him to his granddaughters, already taught by their mother that Grandfather Martin had very impolite ways.

The girls adored the baby at first. He was sweet, a happy mite, laughing at them from the frills and furbelows of his treasure cot.

By the time he was two years old he was a rumbustious lad; and Ellen, used to the ways of daughters, was at her wits' end, as whatever mischief young Joel could find to do he did. He pulled knitting off the needles. He pulled flowers out of the vases, often spilling the water on the highly polished mahogany or rosewood of the tables that were Ellen's pride, as were her flower arrangements. The delicate china ornaments had to be removed, as he grabbed at anything within reach. He refused to be confined to the nursery in the attic; he escaped whenever he could. He pulled the girls' hair, making them scream. He seemed able to get dirty even in an immaculate drawing room. His clothes had to be changed several times a day. Someone was for ever washing his hands, or brushing his hair, trying to keep this wild little boy respectable.

Peter Joel did not want to be respectable. He wanted to be outside in the garden, digging in the soil with his bare hands. By the time he was five he was always escaping from the house through any door he could open, and climbing the trees. He climbed the fence and he fell in the pond; he managed to open the gate and was found riding on the milkman's horse, although nobody could imagine how he had climbed on her back.

Peter Joel grew up sure that the only words adults ever spoke were words of censure. He was for ever being punished; for being noisy, for being dirty, for being disobedient, for being rude. He must not answer adults back. He must learn to be seen and not heard. He must not talk to the tradesmen. He must not trespass in the kitchen.

He was not allowed to play with the neighbourhood boys; they would teach him bad ways. But his sisters' games irked him. By the time he was seven, Louise was fourteen and found a seven-year-old brother a considerable irritation. Helene, at seventeen, was learning to be a lady, her thoughts already on marriage and a home of her own.

The Great War had been raging for almost three years. Grown-ups had long faces and Father, after reading *The Times*, went off to the bank with a very worried expression on his face. Trade was affected, whatever that meant. Peter Joel had very odd ideas about trade. People who were 'in trade' had to come to the back door. That included the odd-job gardener and a disreputable old man who kept a ferret in his pocket and took Joel rabbiting down in the warren, an occupation that Joel was very careful to hide from the family.

By now he preferred to be known as Joel. Peter was a cissy sort of name.

The war ended. The children had been aware of it but it had had little impact on their lives. James David had very bad eyesight which kept him out of the fighting; and Ellen had no male relatives other than her father. The children were sheltered from the news, though Helene, in 1917, had fallen briefly in love with a young man who was killed at the Front. She cried for some weeks, mystifying her small brother who had only vague notions as to what had happened and had no idea at all why it should affect Helene. Joel, trying to cheer her up, brought her presents of frogs and caterpillars, and drove his parents to such a frenzy that he was sent to stay with Grandfather Martin. He was just eight years old.

Grandfather Martin lived at the edge of the moors, near the Welsh border, on an old farm that had been in the family for two hundred years. The house was stone-built, warm, snug against a hillside, with trees sheltering it. There were barns full of hay; there were cattle, with calves, in the fields; there were horses. The paddocks were full of mares, some with foals, and some so fat that they looked grotesque. Grandfather Martin explained that the foal was inside the mare and would be born soon, and the mare would be slim again. At home nobody ever spoke of birth or death to Joel and he was fascinated and wanted to know when the foal would come and if he could watch.

'Reckon so,' Grandfather said. Ellen, he knew, would disapprove, but the lad couldn't be sheltered, and live in a woman's world, for ever. The sooner he learned the better. Grandfather had grown up on the farm; so for that matter had Ellen and how she grew up so prim was beyond the old man's understanding. He had never known that his daughter's first school had been run by a headmistress who was appalled to find a child growing up on a farm where birth and death were everyday facts of life. She had done her best, very successfully, to counteract the evil influences to which this poor waif was exposed. The vicar's wife had taken over where the headmistress left off. Nancy Martin had been city bred; an unwise match for a farmer, but Grandfather had been a handsome man in his time. He had met his wife at a neighbour's house, she having been sent to the country to recover from a winter illness that had affected her health. Grandfather Martin had been bewitched by a pretty face, with lustrous brown eyes and long lashes.

He married her and brought the girl to the farm. She had born him just the one daughter and had then become an invalid, horrified by the facts of birth. Mercifully, she had died. That was almost fifty years ago and she was now barely remembered by her widowed husband.

Grandfather Martin took Joel with him wherever he went: to the beast sales and on a visit to the stallion, when a mare was due to be covered. It was doubtful whether even his farmer friends would have approved of that, but Grandfather Martin saw nothing wrong at all in the daily facts of life on the farm, and regarded his neighbours' pretence that such things did not exist as absurd. He loved the power of his stallions, the power that gave life to the foals within the mares, and surely if God gave such powers there was no need for Man to hide them as if they were indecent? Grandfather revelled in life and he wanted his grandson to learn all he could; the boy was too sheltered at home for any lad and would grow up as soft as a girl if his parents were not careful.

Joel was in the kitchen when the cat had her kittens; he watched each one born, watched the cat purr and lick each clean, removing the clear covering that surrounded each mite. He watched her nurse them and was there the day that their eyes began to open, one at a time, giving each an odd pirate expression.

He was in the pigsty when one of the sows gave birth. He helped the pigman move each tiny piglet and put it to a teat. It did not occur to Walt that the child should not be there. His own son often helped when the other men were busy, and the lad was only a couple of years older than Joel.

Joel helped to muck out the chickens and to collect the eggs. There was no time for mischief of any sort. He was part of the farm, belonging to it, included in everything they did, as were other children, he discovered, meeting the headlad's son swilling down the stable yard with water and brushing it over with a thick heavy broom.

He rode on the carts behind the big Shires. He helped to fill the mangers and hayracks. He learned to clean the harness, to polish the leather until it gleamed. The night before the big County Show he sat up with the men until he was too tired to stay awake, helping to prepare the ribbons and the flags and to polish the horse brasses until they glittered like gold. He fell asleep in the tack room and his grandfather had to carry him up to bed. He did so proudly. This was indeed a chip off the old block.

Joel watched with immense pride as his grandfather was awarded the cup for the Champion and brought it home to stand on the shelf for another year. He had helped to polish it the night before so that it would shine for the new winner. Grandfather had won it the year before, and the year before that.

He was sound asleep the night that Duchess foaled. His grandfather came to his room and shook him awake.

'Want to see Duchess have her foal then?' the old man asked.

Joel was awake in an instant, pulling on his trousers and thick jersey, clattering down the uncarpeted stairs, out into the yard where lanterns hung on hooks, and across to the foaling rooms.

'Not a sound. She doesn't like being watched,' Grandfather said. There was a spyhole in the door. Duchess was circling the stable, pawing the straw; she lay down and her body heaved and heaved again and suddenly a bag hung from it; a slimy dark bag. It fell to the ground and the mare turned her head and curved her neck to worry at it. Within a few minutes the foal lay there, cleaned of his birth bag, his ears flickering. He sneezed, and Grandfather's grin spread over his face until it looked as if it might split his head in two. Duchess stood and bent her head to her foal, nosing him, helping him to try and stand on rubbery legs, watching him as he fell and encouraging him again and again, until he was standing and sucking, her eyes bright with pride at her achievement.

'There's a miracle for you,' Grandfather said. 'She knows just what to do and yet it's the first foal she's ever had. I'll go in and wash her down and you go back to bed, my lad. And Joel, don't you ever tell your mother about this night. She'd be mad enough to kill me if she knew. It's a secret, understand? She's a good woman, your mother, but she never did understand farming.'

Joel understood farming. He understood with a passion that was inherited from the old man; he woke each morning with excitement filling him, never knowing what might happen today. A new clutch of little chicks just hatching out, coming wet from the cracked shells, and drying off, minute creatures so small that to tread on one would be to crush it instantly, yet so full of chirping life. There might be a new calf; a foal in the fields; a litter of little pigs.

Grandfather Martin impressed on him, over and over again, that he must never tell his parents; they wouldn't approve of all that life or of a small son that sat in and watched a birth.

Joel learned early that there were many things he mustn't ever tell his parents. He could not share the joy of racing through the meadows barefoot; of swimming naked in the mill pool, with Grandfather also as naked as the day he was born and the miller encouraging both of them to swim across the pool and back again, until Joel could beat his grandfather and arrive at the far bank to shake himself like the dogs did, and then romp with the dogs to dry himself. His mother did not like the farm collies either; dirty brutes with fleas and worms and they stank, she said.

'Why am I called Peter Joel David and you are called Peter Joel Martin?' Joel asked.

'Your mother was a Martin before she married; and your father's surname is David,' Grandfather said. 'Deep thoughts for a sunny day. Let's see if Kirsty has baked us any scones.'

Kirsty came up from the village each day and cleaned and cooked for the old man. She prided herself on being a decent body and was always away by five o'clock. No gossip about her. She was a big comfortable woman with brown hair and blue eyes that were creased at the corners, with a loud voice and a habit of laughing at herself for being a fool.

'There's scones,' she said, 'and I just stopped myself in time from putting salt in instead of sugar. Proper old fool, aren't I?'

Her rumbling chuckle echoed in the kitchen. Joel loved the farm. He loved Grandfather and Kirsty; he loved all the animals, and he went home with the greatest reluctance.

CHAPTER 4

Peter Joel remained a handful to his parents. They had not been young when he was born and they had no idea how to cope with his energy, his curiosity, his eager explorations that led him constantly into mischief. James David gave up trying to manage the boy he now felt had been born to plague him in his old age.

James was an odd man, believing in demons and sure he must have committed some terrible crime and that this was his just punishment. He had somehow offended God, who had sent his Hounds of Hades to bedevil him, in the shape of Peter Joel. He wanted his son to grow into a good, honest man, a man of whom he could be proud, a man whose adventurous spirit would lead him into playing a role in his country's future. Perhaps a politician, earning high honours; perhaps a leader in the business world, or the banking world. Perhaps an Admiral, or a Field Marshal, saving his country in time of war. A man of whom the world would read in its newspapers, a man of whom his parents would be very justly proud.

James had only a small energy and small ambition, but in the night hours when he lay wakeful, worrying about this son of his, his imagination roamed free. He too was lonely, unable to share his innermost hopes with Ellen. His thoughts would have startled his wife, who occupied her days with busyness, as she began to marry off first one and then another of her daughters.

One wedding and then a second, with two more to follow, made a considerable impact on the family's small finances.

The social round occupied all of Ellen's time. Her son, always in the way, always being told to be quiet, to wash his hands and to keep still, became more and more rebellious. At last his parents decided that they must send him away to school, and allow him to spend his holidays with Grandfather Martin, who appeared able to keep the boy under control.

That was the only occasion on which they took advice from the old man. Joel was sent to a small very minor public school. His parents did not realise that it specialised in educating the sons of wealthy farmers. Grandfather Martin offered to pay the fees.

The school had a thriving Young Farmers' Club. They had their own dairy herd; they bred pigs and cattle; and the boys all learned to ride and hunt. Joel, who had always found his own fascination among the big Shires, now fell in love with his own horse, a beautiful bay mare, retired from racing owing to a leg injury, that Grandfather Martin bought for him. She had won many races as a three-year-old and was bound to produce superb foals, winners on the race-track too. Grandfather Martin restored her to health and gave her to Joel. With her he roamed the moors around the farm; with her he explored the lanes and the bridleways; with her he watched the wildlife that crossed his path, alerted always by her sudden forward-pricking ears and intense stare.

He loved her with a passion that he had never been able to indulge for any human. He tolerated his parents; they gave him little of their time and none of their company; they found fault with everything he did. He was unable to feel much affection for them.

He found his sisters and their preoccupation with

matrimony, silly. Their talk was of clothes and of dances, of trousseaus and bridesmaids. They cooed over babies, and spent long hours closeted in their rooms giggling with their friends, tossing him a casual word if he happened to cross their paths, but mostly ignoring him as a pest and a nuisance. He refused to be page at his elder sister's wedding; and behaved so badly during the week before that he was sent back to Grandfather Martin, who also refused to attend the ceremony (although he sent a cheque for one hundred pounds to the bride). He saw no reason why he should waste his time. One of the cows was due to calve and that was far more important.

Grandfather Martin was a companion, in spite of his age; his grandfather had all Joel's affection, but the mare gave him something he had never known. Not only was she beautiful, but she was his own possession, shared with no one; his charge, his responsibility. He fed her and groomed her and cleaned her stable; nobody else was allowed to touch her and since the boys could bring their own horses to school and care for them there, Sharina came with him. One day, they'd have foals from her.

When he was with her Joel knew a peace that he found nowhere else. The rhythm of grooming her soothed him; the warmth of her body under his hands was a benison, the affection that she gave to him filled an abyss of loneliness that had grown deeper with the years.

He could trust her, as he could never trust a human, for she would not gossip behind his back, or stab him with cruel words or tell him how he had let her down. Even if he betrayed her trust, she would continue to reward him. He could talk to her as he groomed her, tell her the little things that worried him. He could confide in her and know his secret would never be

revealed to any other creature.

By the time he was sixteen his four sisters were all married. They all lived close to the parental home and visited frequently, relying on their mother to help them with the babies that came fast. Joel was an uncle four times over within six years. He went home, briefly, out of duty; he hated the constant feminine chatter; talk of recipes and maidservants and baby clothes; talk of teething, and a house full of silly women.

Nobody had time or the desire to listen to him. His exchanges with his parents were almost non-existent. 'How are you, my boy?' 'Very well, thank you, Father.' 'Could do better at school; must try harder, you know or you won't get anywhere in the world.' Nobody shared his interests. He would never talk to his family about Sharina – she was too precious to share with anyone except Grandfather.

He longed to get back to the farm, to the companionship of the men, to their long talks in the evenings, absorbing knowledge without knowing that he was being taught.

Grandfather Martin enjoyed the boy's company, as he made up for the son that he had never had. Neither realised that the long conversations, man to man, were spoiling Joel for the company of those his own age: he found his form-mates boring in the extreme; he found their preoccupations with food and games and girls childish; he preferred when at school to talk to the grooms, or the gardeners, or the men who tended the animals. His form-mates knew him as a loner, but tolerated him as he was a brilliant rugby player, a magnificent rider and the fastest runner in the school, bringing back all the inter-school trophies for them.

His headmaster worried about him until he learned

from Grandfather Martin that the boy was his heir and would inherit the farm. It was a good farm, a rich farm, and Joel would be better off than many of his schoolmates. There was no further need for concern. The boy took to farming as a duck to water.

Sharina produced a filly foal when Joel was sixteen; a beautiful little creature that followed him like a dog. He felt as proud as if he were its father. One day he would gentle her and ride her too; one day she would have foals and he would sell them. When he inherited the farm he would breed horses. Grandfather Martin nodded his approval. His time was getting short and the evenings sometimes saw him breathless, with a pain in his chest that he knew spelled trouble one day soon. The doctor looked at him and asked his age and nodded. Time was running out.

The Hounds of Hades were at his heels too.

It was an expression that James David had picked up from his wife. It was an expression that was common in the countryside where the old man lived and he used it one night when Joel came in to find his grandfather lying back in his big wicker armchair, gasping, his mouth blue.

'Grandfather.'

'Pills, boy. In my pocket. Water.'

Joel raced to the tap and returned with the glass and watched the old man swallow the pills and sit quiet until the colour returned to his face.

'Old age and rough living,' Grandfather Martin said, as they sat down to the meal which Joel had cooked. 'The Hounds of Hades plague us all at one time or another.'

'Father and Mother say that too. Father, when he was angry, once said I was sent by the Hounds of Hades as his personal devil. What are the Hounds of Hades?'

32

'They say hereabouts that they are personal devils that drive a man to the edge of despair and beyond it to hell unless he has courage to turn and face them and defeat them with his own conviction that life has purpose and meaning. Most people make their own hells, boy.'

'And are they plaguing you now?'

'Only with pain, boy. Time will come; and when it does I'll be glad to go. I'll defeat these Hounds by dying; I have no others now; only those causing pain of the body; you've brought me peace of mind. I know the farm will go on; you'll keep my cattle bloodlines alive; you'll keep it as it should be kept. I've no fears on that score. None at all.'

The old man's words brought comfort to Joel. People rarely praised him; his parents never praised him, and were only free with criticism and blame. Even Grandfather Martin was meagre with his approval.

'It's been a long haul and I'm tired now; almost eighty, and my heart's wearing out, if it isn't already worn out. This will all be yours, boy, and probably sooner than I expected. Take care of it; build on what I leave you; breed your horses; and remember when the Hounds plague you, as they will, that you must fight them. If you don't you'll go under.'

Joel returned to school. One bright morning his headmaster summoned him and told him that Grandfather Martin had died. Joel said nothing. Later that day he went to the farm by train and sat in the stable with Sharina, and only she ever saw his grief. He was alone now, as he had not been alone for years. He was almost seventeen; the farm would be his, and he would do his best by it. He stayed at the farm till after the funeral. He would live there now.

He had reckoned without his father.

The old man's will was an odd one; he had tied up the farm and the income in such a way that nobody but Joel had the use of it. He had, however, omitted one clause from the will: they might not be able to touch the boy's inheritance but they could sell the place. James David was the legal guardian of the boy and the will merely said that he must do as he thought fit until Joel was twenty-one. The old man had not been able to imagine anyone, not even his son-in-law, wanting to sell the farm; he had thought James would install a manager, using the money wisely to pay a good man until Joel was of age. James knew it was ridiculous to imagine a boy of seventeen could work such a place. The old man must have been out of his mind when he remade his will, which was dated only two years before.

Ellen was angry. She had hoped for money from her father and he had not left a penny to her or the girls. Joel must have worked on him. The boy was cunning and wicked. She railed at her son who looked at her, stony-faced, wondering if it were evil to dislike his mother; his sisters raged at him, as they had been sure they too would be remembered. The old man had been very rich. The farm was worth a fortune. It would have to be valued before anything else could be done.

As he was not yet twenty-one, Joel had no say.

It would take time to sell the farm; meanwhile the men would run it and their wages would somehow have to be paid. James David and the bank manager, who was the other executor, were startled to find out how much money the old man had paid for the boy's mare. The old fool must have been besotted. It did not occur to either man that the mare had been an investment for the boy's future; the start of a new bloodline; a breeding line that would one day bring him a fortune. She had been bought after a great deal of research. A foundation mare.

Neither man knew anything about farming. The money from her sale and that of the foal would not only pay the wages for some weeks but also would pay the boy's school fees until he left school.

Joel raged until he was sick with exhaustion, but Sharina and the foal were to be sold. The farm was to be valued and put on the market. It was for Joel's own good. The old man had been too old to understand what he was doing, what a terrible burden he was putting on his grandson, how foolish the idea was. What did Joel know about farming? What could any sixteen-year-old know? It was no use railing. Nobody listened. Nobody understood. Everything his grandfather had worked for would be gone.

Ellen, who had hated the place, was triumphant, and once she knew how much her son cared, was glad to see him suffer. He would have the money; he would be rich while his parents and sisters starved. There was nothing any of them could do about that, but he would not have the farm he had so cunningly connived to inherit, working on a feeble old man who was losing his senses. She did not understand how a son of hers could be so wicked; or how one so young could show such treachery to his family. Disappointment and bitterness sharpened her tongue. She had worked her fingers to the bone for him.

The mare was sold; her foal was sold. They both belonged to Joel and as yet he had no way of stopping the sale. He was under age and subject to his father's rules. His father, talking to a son who was now totally alienated, told him he would be a very rich man by the time he was twenty-one, and as soon as he left school he could learn a good profession, and not bother himself with such absurd ideas now the old man was dead.

35

'A farm indeed. A mere boy, who has no idea at all of anything whatever. You haven't even once brought home a good school report. I had not realised your grandfather had taken leave of his senses in the last few years.'

Joel said nothing; there was nothing he dared say. He longed to take his father by the throat and throttle the life out of him. He went to school. He watched the other boys tending their horses.

That night he ran away.

CHAPTER 5

Joel planned his escape. He had no intention of being found. One day he would return and claim his inheritance; the money that his grandfather had left him. The farm was large; it would surely fetch a small fortune, and on that he would build again and build as his grandfather had intended. Until then he would live as he chose, and he would not, under any circumstances, live the life his father planned for him.

Meanwhile he would learn, and the one place to learn was Newmarket.

He took little with him: a small bag containing a change of clothes and a warm jersey. He wanted to travel fast and light. He had not yet given his term's pocket money to his housemaster to be banked for him. He had five pounds, more than enough to buy him a railway ticket and to live on for some weeks.

A boy of seventeen on his own was unremarkable. He slept behind a hedge, tidied himself up in the waiting room at the railway station, bought a cup of tea and a sandwich and mingled with the market crowds journeying to the next big town.

He stood behind a woman with a big family and offered to hold the baby for her while she bought tickets. She was grateful. None of her sons would even dream of holding the baby. Joel regretted his action as soon as he took over his charge, as it was very wet and began immediately to cry. The ticket clerk and the ticket collector both only saw one boy among several, a boy holding a baby. The boy, to them, was obviously with his mother. Nobody remembered a boy on his own, when they began the search for him.

There were races at Newmarket and the train was crowded with punters. Joel saw a woman struggling with a large suitcase and offered to carry it for her to the cab rank. She was tired and harassed, and told him that her husband had died only a few months before, leaving her with a big stud farm just outside the town. One of her stable boys had left two days before and she had to go and interview several.

'I can't get the type of boy I want,' she said. 'They seem not to care about horses.'

She was a friendly woman and easy to talk to. Joel found himself telling her about his life on his grandfather's farm; and how his grandfather had died and the farm had had to be sold up, as nobody thought him old enough to run it.

'I've nobody now,' he said. 'My parents are dead too. The trustees want to put me to work in a bank. So I've run away. Nobody will care. I'll go back for the money one day; but now I want to work with horses, because as soon as I get my money I'll buy myself another stud farm and run it my way. I'm not working in an office, ever.'

Freda Harris began to question Joel. She was too excited at the thought of a boy who had actually worked with horses to even query his story, or consider the fact that someone might be looking for him. Her grief was too recent; her thoughts were on her responsibilities, which overwhelmed her, as she had had nothing to do with the business side of the stud before her husband's death. He had only been forty-five years old when death claimed him through a heart attack. Since she did not read newspapers she did not see the story of a boy missing from a small public school; the heir to a fortune.

Joel wrote a letter home saying he was safe and well, and they need not worry about him as he was working. He took a train to Wolverhampton, posted it there, took the next train back, and dismissed his school and his parents from his mind.

Life was suddenly exciting. He was with horses; he could ride them, he could groom them, he could feed them; he did not have to go home, away from them, and from the farm, to a sterile city life where the only wild things were small birds and bees and butterflies, and the neighbourhood dogs and cats; where he trod on dirty pavements, and was enclosed by buildings. He no longer had to concentrate on school subjects that he hated. He was part of the adult world, no longer a schoolboy subject to school rules and discipline, nor was he the annoying and badly behaved son of two elderly parents who had no time for him. He was on his own and he was indulging a passion that had been growing slowly over the months spent at his grandfather's farm.

He missed the hills and the forests, but here at least there was open space around him. The farmhouse was modern and neat; the fields flat, divided into paddocks; everything was painted and everything was tidy. He was with mares and their foals all his working hours and had the constant pleasure of learning about each one, of studying the stallions, both of them big handsome fellows with a racing history that gave them a value that made Joel whistle.

Their racing names were too much of a mouthful; their pet names were Cocky and Pain, which was short for Pain In The Neck, as Pain had a nasty habit of nipping anyone standing near him at the back of the neck. Joel found this out very quickly, as he stood too close to the open halfdoor of the stable to put down a bale of hay that had become remarkably heavy in its passage from the haybarn to the stable block. The bruise where the skin was slightly broken reminded Joel for a few days that you never stood with your back to Pain. He might be a beautiful animal, a glorious chesnut and the pride of the stud, producing delightful foals that went on to win their own races as two- and three-year-olds, but he seemed to derive a perverse pleasure from his little habit.

Cocky was a swaggering bay with a knowledge of his own power and he, too, was far from easy to handle.

Joel had told Freda his name was Peter Martin. None of the other stable lads associated him with the newspaper story. The Boss had brought him back with her, and they didn't ask questions. The only lad that ever asked much of Joel was Torr. Torr was Welsh and came from a tiny farm in the hills near the Welsh border. Joel thought at first he was simple, but soon discovered that Torr had never been further than five miles from his Welsh village. The noise and bustle of Newmarket bewildered him.

The other lads teased Torr, but nobody teased Joel. He was solidly built, was already over six feet tall and he had been taught to use his fists. Torr, who was tiny and hoped one day to be a jockey, became Joel's protégé.

Joel joined the stud farm early in May 1926. Life was busy, as there were a large number of foals. His first day was spent holding all those over six weeks old while their hooves were trimmed, and then helping examine all the mares and foals for ticks in their manes and tails.

Freda Harris, who had come out to watch him, was pleased with her new stable lad: he moved gently; he

40

was firm, but also kind, and the foals soon trusted him.

The foals were not yet out at night; but soon they would be and then the work would be easier. Joel was determined to learn all he could and began to keep records; records of the weather; of the work done; of the mares; and which had foals and which were barren; of their colours and shapes and markings; of any odd little ways they had; of their illnesses, and their symptoms; of their treatment.

'Why?' Torr asked one day, coming up to the room Joel shared with another stable lad and finding Joel busy writing in his immense diary.

'Because one day I'll have my own stud farm,' Joel said. 'And this is the way my grandfather taught me. I want to know everything I can about every mare; one day I'll maybe remember something that happened here and it'll help me save one of my own mares' lives.'

Torr laughed.

'And pigs might fly,' he said.

Joel said nothing. He went nowhere; he saved every penny he earned, apart from buying clothes to keep himself decent. He had one ambition now and that was to track down Sharina and eventually buy her back. He could never save up her purchase price; that would have to wait until he was twenty-one and could claim his inheritance. He asked lads from other stud farms and from racing stables if they knew of her, and finally he heard that she was at a big farm about fifty miles away. She had been in foal when sold and her first foal for them was already born; another little filly.

A few months later one of the mares was due to go home and home was on the farm where Sharina now lived. Joel begged to go with her as travelling groom, saying he would like the experience. When the mare and her foal were unloaded and safely stabled, he asked to see round the yard, and found Sharina. She whinnied at him, recognising him, and the need for her hardened into a driving passion. She had been his; his first horse ever; and he had given her all the love that had been pent inside him, all his growing years. She, he thought, had reciprocated; and he wanted her back. He wanted her back with an intensity that was almost beyond sanity. It was a raging thirst for her; a wild craving, a desire that was to motivate him over the years to come, a need he knew to be unreasonable, but that he also knew was going to be satisfied, come what might. He would show his parents; he had no intention of living with them ever again, but he would claim his money in three years' time.

Sharina would then be ten years old; still time for more foals, and foals from her he would have. She had been retired from racing because of a leg injury that left a weakness that returned every time she ran, but that did not bother her in the slightest degree when she was brought to the farm. Her first foal had been born when she was six years old. When he bought her back there would be time for four more foals at least, and then she would live with him for the rest of her life. Joel had everything planned.

It did not occur to him that her new owners might not be willing to sell or that the price might be so high that he couldn't afford her.

It never did occur to Joel that there was any difficulty that he could not overcome.

She was his mare. He regarded her as stolen from him, not sold.

He thought of her often; he dreamed of her at night. He counted every penny he saved, and there was never enough. He lived for the day on which he was twenty-one. He counted the days as if he were in prison, as in a way he was; imprisoned by his own lack of years. He needed to be his own man with his own farm and his own mare.

He wrote in his diary every night; only two years, eleven months and six days; only two years eight months and four days; only two years two months and two days; the years passed too slowly.

He grew into a broad-shouldered very fit young man. His knowledge grew. He picked the brains of every person that would let him, asking endless questions; wanting always to know more and more, unable ever to learn enough, unable ever to save enough, unable ever to grow up fast enough.

Torr, who lived for the day alone, was mystified by Joel. Torr had grown to love the bright lights and the tawdry glamour of the local dance hall, the excitement of the passing girls. He came to life on the back of a horse, his own driving need a need to win, a need to show everyone that for all his small size he was as good as they were. On a horse, he was a wizard. Off a horse, Joel thought him a fool. Yet their friendship persisted.

Torr left the stud for a training yard down the road, and the chance of rides in races. He and Joel met at the Greyhound for an occasional drink, and Joel listened to Torr's chatter of girls, every one the real thing, every one better than the last, to talk of racing and of the horses he was beginning to ride. Joel said little. Had he told Torr of his own obsession Torr would have understood, because his own need to race and win was as great as Joel's need for his lost mare.

Joel confided in no one; he trusted no one; nobody had ever given him any reason to believe that a human being was trustworthy, except for his grandfather; and perhaps Freda Harris, but he was wary

43

even of her, and she, sensing it, never knew why.

He willed the time to pass, but it crawled by, hour succeeding hour, day succeeding day, time creeping on wings of lead.

He had no time for girls. All his thoughts and dreams centred round a chesnut mare with a white star on her forehead and one white sock. A mare he had owned too briefly; a mare he hungered for with a hunger such as he had never known before.

His desire for her became an obsession.

CHAPTER 6

Great Uncle Joel's diaries became almost as much of an obsession to me to read as they had been for him to write. All his life is there; the horses documented in enormous detail; the trivia of his own daily doings and thoughts slipped in, so casually that it seems likely he scarcely realised how much of himself he was revealing by those small, sometimes wry, but extremely observant comments.

In those early years, before he was twenty-one, he reverts constantly to the day when he will go back to his parents and claim his inheritance. 'When I have my own stud farm . . .' 'When Sharina is mine again . . .'

There are paragraphs that show how little anything mattered but the horses. He worked through the day, loving every minute of his time, especially with the foals.

He found it difficult not to waste time watching the mares and foals in the big meadow; the foals kicking up their heels and chasing one another, and then, startled by some terrible sight, such as a rabbit suddenly running across the meadow, they rushed to mother for a quick suck, and for her gentling. Joel always took the long way round so he passed the field gate, knowing that he shouldn't.

In the evenings he preferred to watch a foal being born than to go out as Torr did. One night Torr was off to one of his hops, with the barmaid from the Greyhound, and wanted to make himself pretty, which meant slicking down his hair until it shone as if dipped in goosegrease, and adding a dab of some scent to his unspeakable smart clothes. He thought he looked so wonderful, but everybody laughed at him behind his back. That night he wore a violently coloured check suit and a striped shirt, and his tie needed to be seen to be believed; but the girls seemed to like it. He wanted to borrow money again, but Joel never gave him any.

Joel didn't trust Larry, his room-mate, and sometimes wished he shared with Torr. He put his money straight into a savings account and never kept a penny at the farm, except what was in his pocket. His room was over the stables, reached by a staircase at the back, so that it would have been easy enough to sneak in unseen.

The other lads laughed at Joel because his diary was always with him; or locked, when he wasn't writing in it, in a little case which he left in the Guv's office during the day. Nobody went in there. The Guv laughed at him too; Pete and his diaries; he teased him about recording his lovelife there.

'Do you mean to publish that as a horsey Casanova?' he said. 'Pete's conquests with the girls; they must go overboard for a handsome fellow like you.'

Joel did sometimes take a girl out, but he found them boring; they weren't interested in horses, only in clothes and dancing; and boyfriends. He hadn't time to get mixed up with any woman; not till he had his own place, and had Sharina back. Sharina, who meant so much to him, more than any woman ever could or would.

The Guv seemed to understand. He was a funny little man, a bit like a gnome with a too-big head and enormous feet. He used to be a jockey but he preferred stud work and being with the horses to riding them; he was a wizard with them, nearly as good as Grandfather. He had been there since the year dot, and Joel reckoned he ran the farm even when the Boss's husband had been alive. She asked his advice about everything; she was kind, but a bit silly and didn't know much about horses.

The Guv let Joel stay alone with a mare that was foaling, and only checked twice, asking if everything was all right. It was a long night; Joel had a deckchair and a blanket in the stable next to the mare, and sandwiches and coffee and a big handlamp.

It was a cold, frosty night, although it was May. Joel was used to the stable noises at night since his room was above the horses, but somehow, down here, with the dark outside and everyone else sleeping, it was eerie.

A stamp and a snuffle from the stallion stalls, which were on the other side of the farm, right away from the mares' quarters. Both stallions had been very restless that day and Pain much more of a pain than usual, not only nipping, but trying to get his teeth into the Guv when he led him out for exercise; then he squealed and stamped and put on a bucking bronco act. The Guv just talked to him; soft and soothing, hissing a little, and Pain listened, his ears shifting to catch the sound; and then stood on his hind legs, pawing the air, and only just missed braining the Guv. It took a good twenty minutes to settle the brute. Joel had never met a horse he didn't like before, but on days like that they were all a bit scared of Pain.

Torr was plain terrified.

It seemed only a matter of time before there was a bad accident; he was a nasty animal; thoroughly mean, but his foals were wonderful, and this little one was going to be a winner.

She seemed like his own foal; the first that he'd been allowed to look after without somebody supervising all the time. He spent the night pretending the mare was Sharina and this his first foal at his own stud farm; his winning foal that was going to make his fortune, and make his name; perhaps win the Derby.

He couldn't manage without his dreams. It was lonely without Grandfather and nobody else had ever cared about him.

It was a starry night; bright; with a thin moon, and the frost coming down after midnight. The mare was restless, moving in the straw, rolling, stamping, uncomfortable, once or twice making the oddest noise, a sort of rusty whimper and a panting. She worked at the edge of her box, biting the wood when the pains came; but she never seemed to be frightened; and when Joel spoke she relaxed and looked at him, and let him stroke her neck and talk to her. In the end he curled in the straw of her stall, and kept talking as Grandfather always talked to his mares.

A sudden heave, a straining, and a lifted tail, and the foal slid from her, so fast, and then she was with it, attending to it, licking it, and once it began to breathe, and its ears flickered, she looked down at her baby with that misty look the mares have, and a tremendous pride, knowing she'd done well. Joel told her so as he cleaned her; washed her quarters and removed the afterbirth that came away quickly; put her in the clean stall, ready for her and her baby, as soon as the foal could stagger. Nothing had gone wrong; he had been scared it might, that something awful would happen, something that needed the vet, something maybe he couldn't cope with, and they'd never trust him again.

48

Suppose the foal had jammed and the mare died, and the baby was never born. His mind buzzed half the night with fears.

As it was he felt nine miles high, as if he'd produced the tiny creature. He knew now how Grandfather felt. When a new foal came he'd always say, 'There's nothing like it, Joel. It's a feeling you can never share; only those really addicted to horses ever have it. Either you do or you don't; and when it comes, you'll know it; you'll know the thrill, the achievement, the pride in you, and you wouldn't call the King your cousin.'

As he watched the mare with her new acquisition, he could see Grandfather, standing in the stable beside his favourite mare, Hella. Joel was only a little boy then, and Grandfather was so tall; he thought Grandfather would live for ever. It was impossible to imagine him ill, let alone dying, yet he must have been ailing, even then; they said he had had a bad heart for many years.

He was a big man; much bigger than Joel's father, who was spare, and mean-mouthed, with cold eyes. Grandfather's eyes laughed, and everything amused him; his mares most of all, and his foals. He had a passion for his animals; you don't see it often. The Guv had it, but the other lads didn't care; it was a job, and a hard job, and a mucky job, and a badly paid job, but jobs don't grow on trees any more than money does, and there was no future as jockeys for most of them. Torr wanted to leave and be a jockey and maybe he'd do better at that; he was an odd lad, was Torr.

It was a cold grey dawn, with the frost lying thick still, but Joel was warm with delight. Two animals in the stable today where only one was before and it never ceased to seem a miracle; the mare alone and then this perfect little creature standing beside her, alive, able to see, and soon able to run and buck. He wished he could name her; but the Boss always did that.

Joel watched her move; nothing wrong there; as always, neatly made, delicately built, with that absurd rocking-horse tail, with inquisitive eyes and a questing nose. She tried to suck his finger and then his ear; and he swore the mare was laughing at her.

When he had cleaned up he squatted in the straw to watch them. He was still there when the Guv came. His funny wrinkled face creased even more and he grinned. He had two teeth missing in front, which gave him the look of a very old little boy. He carried a couple of mugs of coffee and a pack of sandwiches.

'Good,' he said, 'Very, very good.'

It was early, two hours before anyone else was due up. He sat beside Joel, cross-legged, looking even more like a gnome, his cap on backwards, the peak down his neck, and he drank in that foal, the way Grandfather used to drink in his foals, revelling in them.

It's hard to describe that look; like the look in Joel's sister's eyes when her fiancé gave her a diamond bracelet worth a small fortune. He could have bought two mares for the cost of that bracelet. Now, a mare is worth looking at; but a pretty bauble that most people think is a fake . . .

It had been a fantastic day. The Boss always came to see the foals; she did love those, although she sometimes seemed a little afraid of horses. She was old now; well over forty, so she wouldn't change. The Guv told her Joel had been up all night and she gave him a pound and sent him off to bed. One pound when he only earned two pounds a week. He must take it to the bank. He hoped Larry wouldn't see it. But at least Larry shouldn't be around during the day; Joel slept with it in his moneybelt under his pyjamas.

Not all Great Uncle Joel's diary entries are so happy. A year later, after writing about the difficulties caused by the general strike, he was writing again of another foaling.

Torr had left by now but he came back briefly one week; he was enjoying riding; and doing well, with quite a few wins and places to his credit. He still wore the most extraordinary clothes. He had inherited his father's cottage and smallholding but had no intention of ever going there, although he said he would keep it as a holiday home. Joel thought he might go there one day; it wasn't more than forty miles from Grandfather's farm.

It was a disastrous day. It started with the new lad tying up one of the mares too tight; she struggled and fell with her head between the manger and the wall and broke her neck. Luckily she was one of theirs and not a mare sent by someone else to the stallion, but that was the only good thing about that. She was a very pretty good-producing mare; a bay with gentle ways; a wonderful mother; and she left a motherless foal.

Luckily too the farm down the road had a hunter mare who had just lost a foal and she took to the baby. The foal was dainty, a tiny filly; and the mare a clod-hopping Irish Shire Hunter cross; they looked so funny together.

That lad only lasted two days; and just as well, as he was stupid and careless and Joel had to do everything he did over again; he wished he'd checked the mare.

'It wasn't your fault,' the Guv said. 'Who could know he wasn't capable of looking after horses? His references were good, but they proved forged.'

As it was, he was sacked too late. Joel and the Guv

sat up all night with one of the most valuable of the visiting mares, from a very wealthy owner in the North. She came to Pain; his progeny were beginning to grow up and make a name for themselves in the racing world.

Joel had checked her at about 7 p.m. and she didn't seem to be breathing right. She was breathing fast and erratic and her eyes looked half wild; she jibbed when he went near, and when he checked her a few minutes later was panting so badly he went for the Guv. He stared at her.

'Damned if I like that,' he said. 'Ring the vet, will you, Pete? Tell him it's urgent. There's something very wrong, and it's nothing to do with her foal.'

Joel went to phone.

Mr Kendal himself answered and said he was on his way. He went back to the stable. The mare was twitching; you never saw anything like it. It was terrible to watch. There was nothing they dared do; they waited for the sound of the car, not speaking, just watching, both terrified. She couldn't do anything now but lose that foal and she was getting worse by the minute.

Tom Kendall came in, took one look at her and said, 'She's been poisoned; that looks like strychnine.'

The next hour was a nightmare. Joel had never seen an animal suffer so and no matter what he tried, nothing worked. In the end her lungs began to pack up; and she had to be put down to save her further agony. Tom operated, but the foal was dead. The Guv stared at her. She was insured, but what kind of reputation would that get them?

Sure enough, the dead mare's owners came down; and there was a hell of a lot of shouting. The Guv had been trigger-tempered and riding everybody rough since it happened. The death of that mare seemed to

52

have broken him up; the police came too.

It turned out the lad that caused her death worked for the mare's owner and they had sacked him for incompetence; he came to get his own back; and as he had a grudge against horses, he did for the mare too; quite deliberately.

Joel had nightmares about that horse rolling in agony; her terrible breathing; her last convulsions and the tiny helpless dead foal. How could anyone harm a helpless animal? What kind of man was he? Only the devil knew.

Suppose somebody did that to Sharina? What kind of people are there in this world? Please, God, keep her safe.

CHAPTER 7

It was a lonely life and a hard one, with the work unending. Joel found his companionship among the horses. His only confidant was his diary. He had never learned to trust people. His sisters had betrayed him constantly by telling tales; his father had been an angry man, asking for perfection from the son he had fathered so late. He had neither charity nor compassion in his make-up. He had been pleased to have a son, but Joel was expected to be a paragon of virtue, to shine at his schoolwork, to behave as his sisters behaved, and be polite and accomplished in society. His mother never recognised that this child was not another girl child and could not be expected to be as gentle or as well behaved as his sisters, all of whom were placid children, with little ambition, and a desire to conform that was nurtured ceaselessly by their mother.

Both his parents were very conventional people, afraid of the neighbours' ever-ready tongues, hiding their own selves in a mass of platitudes and clichés. Ellen, having escaped from the hated drudgery of her father's farm, became more middle class than the middle class neighbours among whom she lived, and determined that her daughters would marry into the professional classes – if she could not marry them, as she would dearly have loved to do, into the County.

Joel was a hindrance to these plans, an embarrassment. He was his grandfather all over again, and she

54

thought her father a terrible man, although she was only too glad when he offered to take some responsibility for the boy.

Joel was passionate, headstrong, with a temper that rose easily to the surface, with a devouring need for justice, for fair play, with an ability to recognise that life was seldom fair to anyone. Joel had grown up without ever receiving praise or kindness from either of his parents, or from his sisters.

The bitterness mounted and crept into his diaries as he neared his twenty-first birthday. He noted his feelings; resenting the family that hated him, resenting the fact that he was an outcast – although he refused to admit that he had cast himself out; or that his parents had not been to blame for his running away. He resented the fact that his parents seemed to care only for his sisters and never for him.

There was no one now to whom he could ever talk freely or trust as a friend. Not even Torr, because Torr drank too much and gossiped when he was among his cronies, bold with too much beer. His admiration for the old man who had been the only human being who had ever shown him care or consideration also crept into his writings. To Joel, his grandfather had been a hero, a man to admire, a man to emulate.

As the days passed, and his twenty-first birthday came nearer, there were more memories of his childhood; as if he needed to whip up anger to face his father, to insist on his rights, as if he were afraid that the money from the sale of his grandfather's farm might not be given to him, even though it was his by right.

On one bleak day, when it had rained without ceasing and they worked soaked to the skin, and he was starting a cold, he wrote not of the horses but only of the past.

Joel's mother had loathed the horses. She had been afraid of the big Shires; had hated their smell and the stench of the muck heap that seemed to permeate the whole farm. She had hated her father's crude language. Her son found her impossible to understand. Sitting, shivering, in the icy room above the stables, blankets round his shoulders, a headache and a sore throat reducing him to utter misery, his thoughts would turn to his life at home.

Little Joel was always being corrected for unseemliness, as if he were a girl, for repeating the words he had heard the servants use when they had not realised he was listening, for tearing his clothes climbing trees, for coming in hot and dirty after trying to catch stickleback in the brook, for being late for meals, because he had been down to the dairy to look at the horses. He revered his grandfather, a man who called a spade a spade, and frequently called it a bloody spade, who let him watch the stallions mating their mares, and the mares foaling, and did not change the subject, with a reddened face, if there were any talk of birth or physical functions.

His mother never admitted there were any physical functions. (Please may I be excused?) And nobody ever admitted to being pregnant even when the baby was so obvious that it looked as if it might be born any minute; Joel couldn't even talk about stallions; that was rude. He wondered how Grandfather ever produced a woman like his mother as a daughter? He never spoke of Joel's grandmother and Joel wondered what she was like.

Joel often wished that Grandfather had waited to die until he was twenty-one and could inherit without need for a guardian. And he wondered why Grandfather made Joel's parents his guardians. Surely he must have known what they would do. But perhaps he didn't know he would die quite so soon; that heart attack had come suddenly, Joel thought.

Joel was vaguely aware of politics; the General Strike of 1926 had affected him only in that it was difficult to get feedstuff for the horses; and the human diet became remarkably plain, consisting for weeks of home-made bread and home-killed pig, and whatever was growing in the gardens.

He was up at five in the morning; with stables to muck out, and horses to groom, and a constant need to prepare food for all the animals; to carry water; to lug straw for bedding; and hay for feeding.

The buckets had to be scrubbed; the floors had to be scrubbed; the yards kept immaculate. Sometimes at night he fell into bed so tired that he could not even be bothered to undress; he slid off his boots, and lay down and was asleep with no time to think, or to hope.

Larry swore and grumbled, but Joel, in most ways, was content. Every day brought him nearer to being his own man; to claiming his rights; to buying back his mare. He saw her several times when other mares went back to the stud farm where she lived, and then, one morning in 1930, Sharina herself came to Pain and was given to Joel's care.

He went to her, feeling like a lover come to greet his girl. Excitement mastered him. He could pretend that she was his again. Would she remember him? He spoke to her and was greeted with an ecstatic whinny, and the dip of her head into his hands so that he held her muzzle. It had been a daily ritual once.

'Anyone would think she knew you,' the Guv said.

Joel was his favourite lad, although he would never show it. The Guv could rely on Joel to do exactly as he was told, to work to the best of his ability, to sit up all night with a sick horse, to care devotedly for an injured horse, to think of ways of making a horse more comfortable, to worry and worry if a horse showed signs of being off-colour, until he came up with a reason. The lad would have made a good vet, the Guv thought. He had a way with horses; a knowledge of them far beyond his years. That grandfather of his must have been a first-class horseman.

'I've met her once or twice when I went to her home with other mares,' Joel said, not wanting to give away any secrets. No one would be looking for him now, after more than three years had passed, but he had no wish to have the stablelads know that he was the heir to a fortune and would soon be in a position to employ any one of them he chose.

Sometimes, when Larry had exasperated him more than was usual, he dreamed of Larry coming to him for a job, begging for work; and of turning him away, and watching the man sidle off, hang-head, turning to plead again, and be rejected yet again. The daydream prevented Joel from venting his frequent exasperation.

Sharina had been sent to conceive her fourth foal. The third was due to be born; and Joel would be with her when she gave birth. Then she would go to Pain and in a few weeks she and her baby would be back on the stud farm where she lived and as far out of his reach as ever. Frustration built up in him, so that being with her was both a constant pleasure and a total misery. She was no longer his. She would go back to the care of other men; perhaps to neglect. Nobody could look after her as well as he could. Perhaps she would return to a lack of understanding. She was a temperamental little mare.

Her foal was due just before his twenty-first birthday; and it was late. There was no way he could leave her. No one else was to be with her when she foaled.

It was his task and his task alone.

He looked forward to it immensely, sure that nothing could go wrong, blithely unaware that his grandfather's hound pack, the devil dogs of misery, the Hounds of Hades, were waiting to bay at his heels.

CHAPTER 8

Joel's twenty-first birthday passed without comment.
He had told no one his date of birth and no one knew
his age. He had a week's leave due to him and
intended to use it visiting his parents and claiming his
rights. But he was not going to leave Sharina with
another man to foal.

Three days after his birthday she seemed restless
and uneasy, and when he went to her during the
evening she laid her head on his shoulder, and leaned
against him, as if trying to tell him how uncomfortable
she felt. He stroked her softly and whispered to her,
as he always did, and she seemed to derive comfort
from him.

He lay beside her as she lay in the straw. It was well
after midnight when the foal was born; not without a
great deal of effort on the mare's part. Joel stood, and
looked down at it. A lusty little colt foal. The foal that
might have been his possession, if his grandfather's
farm had not been sold. The misery that seized him
left him shaking and angry, and feeling a little sick.
Life wasn't fair.

It was never fair.

He cleaned the mare; he helped the foal to stand
and suck; he realised, for the first time, all that he had
been cheated of. His mare, and her foal; the foals to
come; the other foals that would have been born by
now; the farm itself. He would never be able to buy
that back; it would be sold now, in other hands. Only

now did he realise that his dreams had been fantasies, as they had always figured round his grandfather's farm, and round Sharina who now belonged to a man who might never let her go. Her first foal was a four-year-old and was racing now, and had begun to win his races. That meant her price would be very high indeed.

Grandfather had said she would make a dam for racing stock, when he bought her.

Joel sat in the straw and watched the mare suckle her foal, remembering those evenings of bright pleasure, when they had both dreamed of a racing stable, of breeding winners, of making a name. The old man was a wizard with Shires and had bred champion after champion; this was a new field to conquer, a new challenge, and there was nothing old Joel liked better than a challenge.

Now there was a new challenge, but in some way the birth had brought Joel back to earth for the first time, and back to face reality. Reality was that the mare was not his. Reality was that even when he had his money he had to find a base from which to operate. He had to hunt for someone selling property; the property had to be suitable; and had to be well founded. He did not want to spend time building on a derelict place, starting from scratch. There had to be enough money to find a good place.

The mare was doing well; the foal was thriving, and he could have gone to bed, but he could not face the cold bare room, or Larry's stupid remarks, or later, his throaty snoring. It was Saturday night and Larry would be halfway drunk and argumentative.

Joel wrapped himself in a horse rug and leaned against the wall, savouring the mare, and, for the first time in three years, he sat with fear riding him. His parents might have moved and he might not be able to

61

trace them; they might have died, and what then? Could the money have been divided between his sisters? Suppose they thought him dead? How long would it be before they could use his money?

He didn't know. He had never thought about it before. Time had taken so long to pass that sometimes he had thought he never would reach twenty-one. Now he was twenty-one.

The foal flopped into the straw. It had spent the last few minutes trying desperately to stand properly, without rocking on its wobbly legs. It was a beautifully made little creature; long-legged, neatly built, with eyes that turned to look at the man with wonder, finding the world into which it had just come very strange indeed. The mare nosed him and he turned to look up at his mother.

That night grief returned with such force that Joel could not sleep, but lay staring into the dark, his throat aching, his eyes stinging, longing to turn the clock back, for his grandfather to be alive again. Longing for the friendliness of the old farm kitchen, the roof black-raftered, the fire alive, a dancing blaze, with glowing coals. Longing to see again the rosettes and the prize cards on the dresser and the silver trophies in the cabinet, and the dog he had almost forgotten lying at his feet.

He wanted a dog again.
He wanted his freedom.
He wanted his mare.

The thoughts went round and round in his head until he ached with misery. At about four in the morning he turned over, and lay with his arm round the tiny foal, as if that alone could give him comfort.

He woke stiff and aching, his mouth furred, his eyes stinging, and went out into the cold grey morning to start the daily chores. He did not hear Larry come

62

down the ladder from the room above.

Larry had had a bad evening. The girl he had been expecting to meet had abandoned him for someone who was more fun. He sat drinking until the landlord threw him out. He staggered home, bitter and angry, and dropped like a log on his bed, fully dressed.

He woke with a head that pounded at every step and a rankling sense of bitter injustice. He didn't like horses at the best of times, but he did need to work and there were no other jobs for him; he had very few skills. Today he hated the horses.

He had to do Pain first. He didn't hate Pain. He loathed him and the stallion returned the feeling in full measure. As Larry stumbled into the stable, Pain sensed the man's mood, which unsettled the horse badly, so that he lashed out with angry hooves. One forehoof caught Larry on the top of the head and cracked his skull like an eggshell. Larry would never grumble at the world again.

Pain squealed and charged the door and was free.

He hurtled out of his stable just as Joel was leading the mare and foal across to another part of the yard. The stallion skidded to a stop as he saw the mare, but as Joel stepped forward to take his halter, Pain reared again, and squealed again, a mad squeal of rage, and lashed out wildly. One hoof hit the foal on the head, and killed it swiftly and painlessly. The other caught Joel on the shoulder, ripping the skin, so that he stood, pouring blood, sick and shaking, as the stallion squealed yet again and bolted round the yard. If he jumped the gate . . .

The Guv, coming into the yard, found one of his lads dead, the other badly injured, the mare mourning for her lifeless foal, her tongue lick, lick, licking the still-warm body, the stallion berserk, and Joel, in spite of the blood pouring from him, ready to do battle with whoever had let Pain free.

'It was Larry, and he's dead so hold your anger,' the Guv said, feeling ninety years old and beyond coping.

He was talking to no one, because Joel had passed out.

Joel woke to find himself on the settee in Freda Harris's living room, a doctor bandaging his injury, and Freda herself, white-faced, standing by the mantlepiece watching him.

'Sharina...' Joel said.

'The mare's all right, Peter. It wasn't your fault.' Joel, sick and dazed, had momentarily forgotten he was still Peter Martin. Freda watched him with troubled eyes. 'Pain wore himself out and he's back in his stable. He seems little the worse. I wish I knew how it happened.'

'Happens all too easily,' the Guv said, shutting the door behind him as he came into the room. 'Larry had a monumental hangover, the lads say; he was drunk as an owl last night and savage with it. Pain won't stand for a man who isn't in full possession of his senses. It was crazy to even think of going in to the stable in that condition.'

'Larry didn't think even when he was sober,' Joel said, his voice bitter.

'You'll be doing no work with that injury,' the doctor said. 'Rest for at least a week, my boy. You were lucky it wasn't your head too. And lucky that horse wasn't shod.'

No point in saying you didn't shoe stallions. The doctor wasn't interested in horses; only in human flesh and blood, and there seemed a fair bit of that about now. No point in saying anything. What was there to say? He'd lost Sharina's foal and her owners would be asking some nasty questions. He'd failed in his job. He was responsible for the mare and her foal.

64

If only he hadn't led her out just at that moment; if only Larry had been in possession of the few senses he had; if only somebody else had had charge of the stallion.

His grandfather's voice came back to him, a voice from the past, sounding in his head, through a sea of misery.

'If only ... lad, lad, those are the saddest words in the whole of the English language; or any other language come to that.'

'I should have stopped him,' Joel said, coming back to the present with an effort.

'How? Young Pete, the devil himself couldn't have stopped that fellow; he was in a royal rage, and you'd have got killed too. So forget it; nobody's blaming you.'

Later, lying on his bed, his mangled shoulder a burning mass of pain, Joel blamed himself for Larry's death; he had ill wished Larry so often. It was easy, in a bleak mood, to feel that his wishes had come true and fulfilled themselves through the stallion.

Freda Harris brought his lunch up to him herself. She had never been up the ladder and into his room, and when she saw it she was horrified.

'You can't stay here,' she said. 'You'd better come and sleep in my spare room; you're lucky not to be in hospital; or so I thought. I've never been into this room. I'd no idea ...'

Another one who'd never thought, Joel said to himself as he followed her, moving with an effort, his legs shaky as the newborn foal's, down the ladder and across the yard, and dropped, without any sign of gratitude, on to a bed that was fifty times more comfortable than his own bed in the room above the stable and that stood in a room that was handsomely decorated and furnished and warmed by a fire.

65

He spent a painful week, sick and stiff and miserable, with a throbbing shoulder and a high temperature, enduring a half-state between nightmare and reality. He remembered answering questions when the police visited him; but he could contribute little to the story. He hadn't seen Larry that morning; nor the evening before; he had stayed in the stable with the foaling mare all night; he hadn't seen anything until he saw Pain appear like an avenging demon rearing in fury above him, crashing down on the tiny foal.

He saw those killing hooves crushing the life from the newborn colt in nightmares when he was asleep and in a daytime horror that obsessed him when he was awake. It had happened so fast; there had been no time. It had been such a healthy little colt.

It was such a wicked waste.

He felt little remorse for Larry's death. Larry had deserved all he got. If only Joel could be sure that the death wasn't due to his ill wishing. Fever and pain prevented him from thinking clearly. Misery dominated all other feelings. When he was able to move freely again, and he passed Pain's stable, he was appalled to discover himself seized by a fit of trembling and a fear that the stallion would charge out of the stable again and those terrible hooves would drum on his own head.

He remembered asking often after the mare. Freda Harris, sitting beside him one night when he was delirious, asked a question and received an answer that puzzled her for weeks.

'Why are you so concerned for Sharina, Peter?'

'I'm not Peter. She's my mare . . .'

Joel stayed on in his room in her house, and one evening, eating supper in the kitchen with her, where it was warm, with a fire alight and the cat lying at ease on the hearthrug, Freda returned to her own puzzle.

'You said your name isn't Peter,' she said.

'I'm Peter Joel,' Joel said. He was relaxed and comfortable, at ease for the first time for a long time, and full and sleepy and off-guard. He told her the secret that he had been hiding for more than three years. She listened, saying little.

'The Guv said you knew that mare extremely well. He's been wondering,' Freda said.

'I felt as if she'd never been away. I used to go and see her when I went up to Mainwell's; I found her on that first visit. One of the lads in the pub told me where she was. He had been working there.'

Freda looked at him, her face thoughtful.

'May I tell the Guv? It would set his mind at rest. He's been dreaming up all sorts of discreditable stories about you. He thought you were running away from the law, and maybe liable for a prison sentence. You are such a clam. You've been our stable mystery man, Peter. Or do I call you Joel?'

'Suit yourself,' Joel said. It no longer mattered.

'Will you be going to see your parents soon?'

Joel nodded. He didn't confess that he was scared; scared that something might have happened to them; or to his inheritance; scared that it might after all be a small sum and not a large one; scared that he might have no future at all, other than to work for the rest of his life in other people's stables, with other people's horses; that Sharina might never be his again.

He spent much of his time with her. He couldn't yet use his right arm; he could soothe her and supervise the lad who looked after her; he could stand beside her and mourn with her for the small life that had lasted such a short while.

'Will you come back to us while you are hunting for your own place?' Freda asked.

67

Joel doubted that. He was unable to overcome his fear of Pain.

At last the doctor said he was fit to start work again. He packed his few belongings into a suitcase and said goodbye to Freda and the Guv. Sharina had already gone back to her own home, after her visit to Pain. The insurance had covered the loss of the foal. Nobody had made a fuss. It was one of those things, her owners said, knowing that accidents happen on the best run farms, when livestock was involved and stallions could be chancy beasts. He had said goodbye to Torr the night before in the Greyhound and Torr had offered him the use of his own home in Wales while he was hunting for somewhere to live.

Rough and ready, Torr said, and only occupied very rarely; nobody lived there now, and Torr seldom went home. Perhaps an odd weekend with a girl; and one or two weeks of holiday. When he left Joel had the key in his pocket; Freda had given him a bonus, and had offered him his job back any time he wanted to come.

He sat in the train, watching the fields speed past; watching the towns flash by, retracing the journey he had made over three years before, back to the home he had left without more than a brief note to say he was well, and for the first time he wondered just how they would greet him.

He bought a paper and read the racing news. He hardly noticed the front-page headlines: something about the terrible state of the economy continuing.

The words meant nothing to him.

CHAPTER 9

Nothing had changed.

The street was the same. The neat houses; the neat gardens; the trees were a little higher; the bushes bigger; the paint on his own home shabbier. Joel stopped at the gate and looked at the net curtains hiding the rooms inside. His mother had always regarded net curtains as a sign of extreme respectability. There had been no net curtains on the farm. The kitchen windows there had been curtainless. The curtains had worn out and Grandfather Joel had never replaced them. Why should he bother with such frippery? They only got dirty and needed a wash.

'I've nothing to hide, boy,' he often said, and laughed the big rumbling belly laugh that always made Joel laugh too, even when he couldn't see the joke.

Joel had deposited his suitcase at the left luggage office. He stood now at the gate. A neat wrought-iron gate with the house name written on it in curly letters. Dunroamin. His parents hadn't named the house. He looked at the name and wondered what they would have chosen. Something very similar, he was sure.

What should he say? How did you return after so long? Would they even let him in? He had not eaten any breakfast; he now felt sick.

He walked up the path and rang the bell.

It seemed an age before anyone answered, and then, to his surprise, it was his eldest sister, Helene, dressed in black, looking more than three years older. She looked at him without recognition.

'I'm Joel,' he said.

'So you turned up for the funeral. I suppose you thought there would be pickings,' Helene said, and Joel stared at her without comprehension.

'Whose funeral?'

'Father's funeral. It's tomorrow. I don't know if mother will want you there. She's upset enough without you adding complications.'

Joel pushed into the hall, and closed the door behind him. Nothing had changed. There was the big hall stand, with its polished table on which the phone stood; the mirror in which he had looked to set his school cap straight; the elephant-foot umbrella stand; the brass barometer on the wall; the picture of the Monarch of the Glen in its gilt frame; the brown dado and the cream paint; the patterned flowery frieze under the picture rail. Time had stood still here, while he had gone on. He felt like a little boy again, jolted back to another age; a small boy, waiting to hear an angry roar because he had done something wrong again. Now his sister stared at him accusingly, her eyes angry.

'Why have you come?'

'I'm twenty-one. I came to claim the money from Grandfather's farm,' Joel said.

Unnervingly, Helene began to laugh. The shrill sound echoed through the room and brought his other sisters running. Suzanne, after one amazed glance at Joel, slapped her sister's face, guided her to a chair, and poured out a glass of brandy and gave it to her.

'Joel's come for his money,' Helene said.

Four pairs of eyes stared at him as Louise's husband came into the room.

'You picked your time,' he said. 'OK, girls. Off with you. Let me talk to Joel. I hope Mother didn't hear that din; she's had enough to put up with.'

The four women left, with only Suzanne giving Joel a backward glance. To the others he might not have existed.

Richard Tate went to the table and poured two glasses of whisky. Joel had never known his brother-in-law well. He looked at him now; a big man, dark, with an easy manner, but with a strained expression on his face.

'Where have you been all these years, young Joel?'

'Working with horses, near Newmarket. Learning. Ready for getting my own farm,' Joel said.

Richard Tate walked to the window, and looked through the whisky in his glass at the curtain as if there was some kind of answer there to a problem that was bothering him. The silence lengthened, until Joel was so on edge that he swallowed his whisky fast and poured himself another.

'That might soften the blow,' Richard said.

'Soften what blow?'

'There isn't an easy way to tell you,' Richard said. 'I had hoped you'd dropped out for good; maybe emigrated, and begun to make your own way in life without counting on your grandfather's money.'

'What's happened to it?' Joel could barely speak. He saw all his nightmares coming true.

'The same thing as happened to all our money; the bottom dropped out of the market; we're all paupers, young Joel. We don't want to be. But there it is. We invested, we all thought wisely, and your father invested your money too. The market crashed. Your father finally committed suicide. He shot himself. We didn't even know he had a gun. Men have committed suicide all over the world. Vast fortunes have been

71

lost as well as small ones. He's just one of many. None of us has a penny; and there's nothing left of Grandfather Joel's farm money. It's gone; you never had it and you never will. I don't think it would be a good idea to stay on; I don't think your mother could bear to see you. She hoped you would never find out; there's been a lot of bitterness already over that legacy of yours. I know the old man meant well, but he didn't think about his own daughter.'

'She didn't ever think much about me,' Joel said.

He had waited; he had planned; he had never contemplated being penniless. He didn't want to see his mother; he did not care how his father had died. He was aware of growing fury, fuelled by drinking whisky on an empty stomach, of a deepening of an emotion that he now knew to be hatred. He wanted to get away, on his own, away from the family that had neglected him, that had taken his money and lost it for him.

Richard Tate stood there, watching him, not knowing what to say, wishing that time had rolled back and they were all wealthy again. He had his own battle to fight; his own way to make and two children of his own to bring up. They had had to make sacrifices: the children had to leave their schools; they had moved to a cheaper house, without servants.

He was aware of the surging fury that dominated Joel.

Joel could say nothing. He wanted to lash out at someone, to fight and cleanse himself of the sick anger that possessed him. He blundered out of the room, through the hall, and into the street. He wanted nothing to do with any of them. He was never going to see them again. He was glad his father was dead and a moment later sorry, as he would have liked to meet the old man and rail at him, vent his fury on him.

72

Now there was nobody he could attack.

Had he stayed he would have hit out at his brother-in-law; and that wouldn't have been fair. Even in his confusion and misery Joel had recognised that Richard had done his best; had tried to be sympathetic; had not known how to break the news or ease the pain it caused.

There was nothing to do but walk; walk with anger choking him; walk through the streets at a pace that frightened some of those who met him; walk with clenched fists and a set face and a desperate need to work off the helpless rage that mastered him.

He walked blindly, seeing nothing, driven by anger so great that he did not know how to contain it. He ignored those who passed him, so that they had to jump out of his way, or he shouldered them, unaware of their presence. He walked through long streets and turned into narrow cobbled alleys.

Once he passed a Salvation Army man, who looked at him and spoke.

'Are you all right, son? Can I help?'

Joel walked on, not bothering to answer.

Once a policeman looked at him, about to speak and decided it might be wiser to hold his tongue. He watched the striding figure until it was out-of-sight.

Rain began, first a thin drizzle and then a downpour. Joel ignored it; ignored his sodden clothes, ignored the hair that was pasted against his cheeks, ignored the puddles, splashing through them.

As he walked his feet beat out a rhythm. No money, no money, no money. He had lived all this time with hope; he had worked; he had dreamed; and now there was nothing. He was overwhelmed by despair, by sick misery. He had planned for so long; and now he had nothing. Nothing. Nothing.

And Sharina was further away than she had ever been.

Day turned to dark. Gaslights lit the streets and reflected in the puddles. A cat ran past him as wet and draggled as he. He was hungry.

He turned into a small cafe, where the surroundings and staff smelled of defeat, and sat at one of the tables, unaware of the dirty floor, the stained cloth, and the debris of other people's meals around him. The waitress was a slut, smelling of stale sweat, her dirty bare feet thrust into broken shoes. She had greasy hair and an overall that should have been washed a few weeks before. He ordered baked beans on toast and coffee. The beans were cold and the coffee was vile.

It didn't matter. Nothing mattered any more.

He paid and went out into the night. The rain had stopped. Ragged clouds scudded across the moon, and the wind was rising. It drove him, whipping at his hair and his clothes, and he walked on, knowing that the Hounds of Hades were at his heels, and would drive him for ever. He was haunted by his grandfather's demons; the demons of despair.

The road ended abruptly at the riverside. He stood staring at the sluggish water. There lay peace; there lay escape; there lay the end of all hope. There, for a moment, he recognised the demons that had driven his father and caused him to take his life.

Almost, he felt pity.

Then pity was surprised by disgust. His father hadn't had the guts to stay and fight the world. The Hounds had driven him to the brink and beyond, but they would not drive Joel. He was his grandfather's stock. The old man would have fought like hell.

Joel turned his back on the water. Somewhere, far away, a clock struck eleven. It was late and he was cold and had nowhere to sleep, and no desire to waste his money on any kind of lodging. He needed every penny he owned, and more beside.

He walked on. He had no idea where he was. The cobbled streets were entangled, spreading in all directions; the houses small and mean. They were streets of despair. Streets of desperate poverty, where people strove to live as well as they could. A girl passed him, running, casting a glance of fear over her shoulder, and then relaxing, and walking, though fast, as he made no attempt to speak to her or follow her.

He was hungry again.

He turned a corner and saw light spilling out through the arched doorway of an old stables. A brewery stables, he guessed. A moment later he heard the stamp of a horse in the straw, a soft whinny, and a man's voice speaking, and then a sound that he knew all too well; a mare coming to birth and trouble in her voice.

He walked inside. There were horses in stalls along the side of an immense barn. At the far end a lamp shone, and the sounds came from there. He went to the isolated stall. A small elderly man, his face dark with effort, was trying to bring a foal from a big Shire mare; only the hindlegs showed.

'Vet's miles away.' The man paused and turned his head. He had obviously been expecting someone else. 'Who the hell are you?'

'I was passing; I heard her. You need help. Come on. Or that foal'll suffocate; maybe two of us can do it. If the vet can't come we've no choice.'

They took a hindleg each. The mare was a veteran and had foaled before; the passage was enlarged, and the two men, pulling as the mare struggled, felt the foal move; it slipped out and they caught it, and laid it

75

in the straw. Joel pulled away the membrane, and watched for life; there was none. He grabbed the foal and shook it; he pumped at its ribs, and then began to rub it, and the mare, turning towards her offspring, began to lick too.

The foal sneezed.

'Thank God for that,' the man said. 'You saved my bacon, mate. The groom's drunk. I don't know much about horses. I only clean up around here and look after the place at night. I sleep in that little room; but I couldn't leave her, could I?'

The little room was a cubbyhole off the stables. They passed the groom, a fat man with a beer belly, lying snoring in the straw.

'The mare needs food; and cleaning up,' Joel said. 'Know how to do it?'

The man shook his head.

'Been my job for almost four years. Get me some food and a hot drink and I'll do it for you; you can pay me with food, and a chance to kip in the straw when she's tidy. I've nowhere to sleep tonight.'

The jobs were familiar; clean straw, and a clean mare rewarding him with a nudge of her nose, as he lifted her baby, to shift it into another stall where everything was fresh and sweet. He made her a bran mash and filled the rack. It was a well-found stables, except for its groom.

'He reckoned she wouldn't foal till tomorrow; he might have stayed sober else,' the old man said. Joel was not happy with the mare; she had had a hard time. He put hot fomenations on her and covered her with a rug and then a blanket which he stitched in place. It was necessary to keep her warm. He thought of Freda's superbly run establishment; she would have been appalled by this.

There was a campbed in the old man's room, as well as a shabby battered armchair. There was a gas ring, on which he heated a pan of soup and gave a bowl to Joel when he came in from the mare.

'I kip by day, so you can lie there and welcome,' the old man said. 'I can watch the mare. I'll call you if anything looks wrong. Get those wet clothes off, mate, and dry them by the fire. The blankets are warm, and I ain't got nothing wrong with me except age. And that's incurable.' He chortled suddenly.

Joel thought he could never sleep, but he was asleep within seconds, exhausted by the varying emotions of the day. The room smelled of horses; the familiar smell of warm clean horse at night; of clean straw. The place might not be first class, but it was as good as it could be under the circumstances.

He woke to the sound of men's voices. The room was empty. His clothes were dry and laid out on the armchair. He dressed hurriedly, not wanting to be caught at a disadvantage. A black cat was lying in front of the small coal fire, licking herself clean after her nightly adventures with the rats. She was heavily pregnant.

The groom came into the room, surly.

'I 'ear you saved my bacon,' he said. 'What are you after? If it's my job, forget it.'

'I was passing,' Joel said. 'I don't want your job. I've got my own job. Just a helping hand.'

The man went out, and the watchman came in.

'I'm off-duty now, mate' he said. 'There's a good little place for breakfast, and then it's me for bye-byes. You off after that? Boss heard as you'd helped and he's standing you your grub and a quid beside. He likes 'is mares and foals, does the Boss.'

77

Joel went to look at the mare and found an emaciated elderly man standing beside her, giving her sugar lumps. The foal was feeding; a sturdy little filly, with massive hooves.

Joel grinned at it. It was nothing like the racehorse foals he was used to; its chunky body moved as he came to look at it, and he reached out a hand to stroke the soft neck. The groom came into the stall with a bucket of fresh water.

'Thank you for helping Ted last night,' the stranger said. 'He tells me you had quite a time pulling the foal clear.'

'Took us near on an hour, didn't it, mate?' the groom said, his eyes daring Joel to refute the lie.

'I was afraid we'd damage her,' Joel said, seeking refuge in the literal truth. He had no desire to stand up for the man, and he despised a man who could get helplessly drunk when he had such a charge.

'The veterinary came while you were asleep. Says you both did a good job. You looking for work?'

Joel shook his head.

'I've my own place,' he said.

He thought of Torr's cottage. It would be a refuge and give him time to think; he needed to be away from people. He needed to make plans. If he started work for someone else he would be trapped for ever.

He wasn't going back to Freda with his tail between his legs, begging for a job. He wasn't working for anyone else, ever again.

He thanked the man for his bounty and went outside to join the old watchman, to eat bacon and eggs in clean surroundings, with good hot coffee, and then he set off to walk to the railway station, reclaim his baggage, and take the train to Wales.

The train's wheels sang a new litany.

Sharina. Sharina. Sharina.

He did not realise, then, or in the future, that the Shire mare's difficulties had saved his sanity that night.

CHAPTER 10

Torr's cottage was situated some way from the village. The village itself was five miles from the only station. Joel arrived just before 4 p.m. and walked the five miles. Anger drove him so that he walked fast, arriving at the little village post office ten minutes before closing time.

It seemed to be the only shop. A small shop with two big windows filled with notices about posting times, closing times, and several handwritten posters in Welsh, presumably advertising forthcoming village events.

Joel went inside, and as the tinkling bell stopped a raucous voice shouted 'Shop.' There were noises from the back room but nobody appeared, and the voice said, 'Two penny stamps, please.' It then chuckled and added, 'Bore da, cariad.'

Baffled, Joel looked about him and then grinned as he saw a large cage on a wide shelf above his head. The cage was flanked with big glass jars of sweets; bullseyes and humbugs, peppermints and bright-coloured gobstoppers; long sticks of black liquorice. In the cage was a grey parrot, regarding him with a bright inquisitive eye. It yelled 'Shop' again and an elderly man came through the door behind the counter. The parrot navigated its cage, carefully, walking up the sides, along the top, hanging downwards, trying to see over its head, and then returned to its roost and announced loudly, 'You're stupid!'

'Just having a cup of tea,' the postmaster said. 'Sorry if I kept you. Don't usually get anyone in at this time. They're all preparing tea. Can't seem to move the way I used to before.'

Joel had expected a Welshman, but this man plainly was not Welsh.

'Susie always tells me when the customers come.'

'Poor Susie's lonely. Tom's dead,' the parrot said, in a pathetic voice.

'Tom died donkey's years ago,' the postmaster said. 'He was my son. Killed on the Somme. Susie was his parrot. Can I help you?'

'I'm looking for a cottage called Llain Grin. Do you know it? I'm a friend of Torr's; he says I can use it for a bit.'

'Out of work?'

'Not exactly.'

Joel thought. The village would be curious about him, and he didn't want to arouse curiosity.

'I'm getting over a bad injury. I was kicked by a stallion. I work with horses. And my father died; he was buried yesterday. I just want time to sort myself out and get strong again. No use working with horses unless you're fit.'

'It comes to us all, but it's never easy to come to terms. God moves in mysterious ways, and takes the best of us,' the old man said.

'Shop,' said the parrot, and screamed unnervingly, then shook its feathers, and resettled on its perch.

'Daft, that creature is, but it's company since my wife died. And tells me who's about. You'll be needing food; there's no other shop near the cottage. You won't find much there; it's mostly empty these days, since old Jim Torr went.'

Joel hadn't thought about food. He was grateful for the suggestion and bought bread, butter and cheese;

sausages and tea and milk, eggs, bacon and a pound of apples. The old man lent him a clean sack to carry the goods.

'Bring it back when you come again,' he said. 'Go out of the shop now, turn right, and right again at the end of the lane; over the little bridge, it's a humpback, and it's the second cottage on your left. Quite a walk; nearly two miles I'd guess.'

Joel walked past fields in which sheep were pastured; a field of black and white cattle; a field where two horses grazed. He stopped to look at them longingly. A child ran past him, bowling a hoop, and another child was whipping a top in a garden. A small girl in a blue gingham dress stared at him through a garden gate, sucking her thumb.

Then there were no more houses.

The lane was narrow. A farmcart passed him, the big horse plodding, its muscles straining. There would be few cars here. The farmers used horses for ploughing; he might get an odd job with a man with several horses, just to take his mind off his woes. Maybe there would be a horsebreeder round here who needed a man. Torr hadn't put any time limit on his stay.

There was a small board saying Llain Grin; at the start of a long lane that looked like a cart track leading to nowhere. Joel turned into the lane, which was rutted and muddy, water lying in puddles, the centre grassy. He passed a field of shaggy sheep, and a field of growing crops that might be turnips and came to a five-barred gate.

A narrow drive, that seemed to be made out of bedrock, led downwards. He could just see the cottage chimneys.

The cottage itself was larger than he had expected, built of stone. The recessed windows had sills that were two feet thick. The building was whitewashed, and endearingly irregular, the lower part of the walls projecting, apparently carved out of the rock.

Joel put the key in the door and opened it with difficulty. It was an oak door, thick and heavy, which led into a stone-flagged passage. There were no lights. Joel, used to gaslights, realised he would now have to learn how to use oil lamps. An oil lamp stood on a table in the passage, which was too narrow to be called a hall. His parents, he realised suddenly, had installed electricity, which was just beginning to be used instead of gas. He had noticed the central lamp and the switch without realising what he was looking at. Freda had talked about changing over, but had not yet done so.

Joel felt uneasy, exploring another man's home in his absence. The living room was unusually large and must have been made from two smaller rooms. Beyond it was another room, with a wood-burning stove for cooking, and beyond that a kitchen that must once have been a dairy, leading from it by an archway. There were dirty dishes in the deep brown sink, and on the stained wooden table was a mouldy loaf, the crumbs spread around, mingled with mouse droppings, and half a bottle of very sour milk, also crusted with green mould.

The stone walls bulged, and no wall seemed to be straight.

A doorway opened onto narrow stairs leading upwards into two bedrooms, one leading from the other. Torr had not tidied here either. The unmade bed was covered with dirty calico sheets, and there were two cups, holding the stale dregs of long-ago drinks, standing, saucerless, on a small table by the bed. There was dusty water in the big china jug that stood, in a matching flowered washbasin, on the marble-topped washstand.

The second room held a brass bedstead, the bedding neatly folded. Joel found clean sheets in a cupboard; they felt damp and he thought longingly of a fire and warmth. Before he went downstairs again he made up the bed. There was an almost unused candle in a brass candlestick on the bedside table and he took it downstairs with him when he went out of the room.

There was a handlamp on the kitchen dresser, which he lit and took to explore outside. He found a logstore in one of a rank of dilapidated stables. The whole place was bigger than he realised, and there were a number of ramshackle outbuildings. He was too tired to explore these as well, and his shoulder ached badly.

He needed to find the lavatory. He investigated several sheds before he discovered it. He stared in disbelief, as the only facility consisted of a wide plank with a hole in it, fixed over a gully, that, from the noise, dropped, far below, to a rushing stream. He hoped the stream wasn't the source of his drinking water. The floor of the little cubbyhole was hard earth.

Indoors once more, he found a fireplace in the living room, a hob attached to it, on which stood a blackened kettle. Joel had to clean out the ashes. He longed for the comfort he had known briefly at Freda's home while he had been ill. He wanted water to make a hot drink, but there was no indoor tap.

The piles of newspaper that he found beside the kindling wood were damp; the wood itself smoked and smouldered and the logs refused to burn. Joel put his overcoat on, and sat in a big wicker armchair that creaked whenever he moved, and ate buttered bread and cheese, and drank cold milk.

Later, lying on the lumpy bed in the spare room, he watched clouds torment the moon and hide its face, and thought of the devil hounds chasing him to hell, and knew such desolation that he wished he had succumbed to temptation and ended his life in the river.

He could go back to his old job, but he wasn't going back. Perhaps he should emigrate, but if he did he would lose Sharina for ever. He intended to buy the mare back. He didn't want any mare; he wanted his mare. He wanted her because he loved her; he wanted her because his grandfather had bought her for him; he wanted her to spite his father.

He wanted to be able to go to his father's grave and stand on it and yell at the dead man, as he had never yelled at the living man.

'I got her, in spite of you, you old devil.'

He fell asleep at last, but sleep brought little peace, as he dreamed that he was standing beside Sharina as she gave birth; and the foal she bore was deformed, a twisted ugly creature, that died as it was born.

He woke unrefreshed with an aching head, and a wish that he could go downstairs to a cooked breakfast and a glowing fire; to someone who would comfort him and talk to him and encourage him.

The feeling passed, as he had become used to a hard life. The men at Freda's led a spartan existence. His bedroom had been bare and cold. The food was adequate but never very well cooked, as few cooks liked the conditions and few ever stayed. Nobody complained. A job was a job and work was scarce.

Later that day Joel explored the bookshelves. There were few books but they would occupy him for a day or so. He felt drained of all energy, wanting only to sit and brood. Nobody would bother him here. He needed to be alone. He would be poor company for anyone.

He looked out of the narrow window, at fields that

sloped upwards to the skyline. At shaggy massed clouds that threatened rain soon. At neatly laid hedges, cut trim. At the stream, within sight of the cottage, running fast and clear over tumbled boulders. There were trees on the horizon, twisted with the wind. There were fields all round him. It would be a good place to live.

The filthy house offended him and he used his anger to goad him to tidying, until it looked as it must have looked when Torr's parents were alive. He emptied the stale water from the jug and filled it with fresh; he found soap and towels. He cleaned the kitchen and scrubbed the floor and table. He cleaned the cupboards. The dirty remnants of old newspapers, used as lining, offended him. He would buy newspapers and reline the shelves. His grandfather might not have worried about curtains, but the house had always been clean, the windows sparkling, and Joel, when he stayed at the farm, had to turn to and work as well. Grandfather never allowed passengers.

Freda's stables had always been immaculate, and he had kept his side of his own room tidy. Larry had been bad enough as a room-mate as he was very untidy, but Joel knew now that he could never have shared with Torr. Larry had been irritating and careless; he hadn't been filthy.

It took two hours to tidy the bedroom; to sweep the floor, raising dust from the worn carpet that made him choke; to wash the furniture; it needed that before polishing. There were rings, left by numerous cups, on the bedside table. It was irritating work but far from tiring to a man used to caring for horses.

By late afternoon the house was clean; the fire was blazing. Joel had comfort at last. All the chores were done. The lamps were ready for the night; he found a store of candles, and, just before dusk, walked to the village and bought paraffin and kindling wood. He also asked for all the day's newspapers.

'Going to read them all?' the postmaster asked.

'Read, read, read,' shouted the parrot.

'I want them to light the fires,' Joel said. 'All the paper there is damp.'

'It would be. The house is empty for too long,' the old man said. 'You don't want to waste your money on newspapers. I've a huge pile of old ones here; people bring them, as I use them for wrapping soap and candles and firewood. You're welcome.'

Joel took the proffered papers, and bought a mousetrap as well; he had no desire to share his home with the dirty little beasts, even briefly. He tramped back through the dark, along the deserted lanes, passed only once by a man leading a wearily plodding horse. The man nodded and spoke briefly in Welsh. Joel, interpreting correctly, said goodnight.

He walked on, listening to the night sounds. He was not used to isolation such as this. An owl hooted and was answered; a sheep bleated, and, far away, sounding clearly on the air, a cow, calving, bellowed her discomfort.

Tomorrow he would hunt the hedgerows and find sticks with which to prime the fire. He was husbanding his money; buying frugally, aware that with every mouthful he ate his ambitions were being destroyed, penny by penny.

He did not rest until after his tea, when the dishes were clean and tidied away. The curtains were drawn, and the room was a sanctuary, cosy with firelight.

He slumped, feet to the blaze, trying to plan his future. It had to be a future with his own stud farm; somehow. He didn't know how. It had to be a future which included Sharina. Somehow. He didn't know how.

He had to keep both ideas firmly in his mind, and

work towards that and plan towards that. Sharina was now ten years old; he wanted at least four foals from her, maybe more, and he wanted her to end her life in his care; to repay her for the immense pleasure she had given him in the days before his grandfather's death.

He was no longer interested in making money from her foals. He craved her for herself. If only he had her he could make a life of sorts here. He felt as if his inheritance had been a dream, the money only fool's gold. Dozing, he saw his grandfather standing above him as he lay on the ground, thrown and then kicked by one of the more frisky ponies.

'Get up and get on again and don't lie there feeling sorry for yourself,' the old man had said, 'God's no time for miseries.'

God had been grandfather's authority, and a very strict God he had been, Joel thought, with no time for gossips, or frauds, or cheats, or liars, or fools, or dirty habits. Grandfather's God hadn't much time for men who were cruel to animals, or didn't know a thing about horses, or didn't use the brains that He had given them.

The other thing that Grandfather had said was that when great decisions had to be made, it was best to sleep on them, to take time and not force them, and then God would show the way. When one door closed, another door opened. Grandfather had smoothed life's path with his platitudes.

Money isn't everything. Peace of mind comes first.

Work was the best drug there was, Grandfather had said.

Joel picked up one of the old newspapers.

He had been unaware of the existence of the Stock Market, except as a vague institution that other people used money to invest on. Freda had spoken of it as a mug's game once; her money was in horses, or in the bank. She had confided in him, a little, while he had been convalescing. Now, sitting alone by the fire in a strange place far away from everyone he knew, Joel realised that Freda had been desperately lonely. She had had to build her life again after her husband's death.

Death. He wondered briefly if his father had gone somewhere else; had a chance to look back over his past life and regret some of his actions; to regret the son he had never known and never cared about; to regret the way he had misused the money. The rage was dying, followed by a frightening feeling that Joel had almost ceased to exist; he was disorientated, divorced from reality, sitting in a fog of misery that refused to clear.

If only he had Sharina, life would seem worth living again. Now, he stared in to the flames, and saw pictures of desolation. All his hopes had been burned away, as the wood was burning away. Nothing was left but ashes.

The paper was an old Sunday paper, which contained numerous long and detailed articles analysing the consequences of the collapse of the financial system in America. He read, for the first time, of the gambling fever that had swept the United States; of the little men in offices everywhere, and the big speculators, borrowing money they didn't own to invest in shares that were only theirs on paper. They had no money to buy them. They only needed to put down ten per cent. If the shares went up they made a fortune; if the shares went down they had to pay with money they didn't have for the vast sums they had gambled on owning. It was the biggest and most widespread gambling in history. This time the shares had gone down and down, until they were worthless;

everybody selling and nobody buying. Men had sold fortunes for a few cents in America; men had killed themselves.

It had been unprecedented; and his father couldn't have known what would happen. Nobody could have guessed; six months before, all would have been well.

It was a worldwide disaster; one that had caught him and thousands of other people, whose dreams had been destroyed in a week of unprecedented madness. But the trouble had begun when his father had sold the farm; that should never have happened, and the old resentment took hold of Joel, so that he paced the room, restless and angry, not knowing how to use the energy that was driving him.

He took pencil and paper, and tried to work out his finances. Freda had been a good employer. He had earned eight pounds a month; and banked five pounds each month. Freda paid for their keep. He had no rent, and no food to buy. In the more than three years he had been there he had saved one hundred and fifty pounds. It wouldn't buy the farm he needed. It wouldn't buy the horses; it might not even buy Sharina. Her foals were already beginning to win the big races.

Torr had said that he didn't want rent. He'd be glad to have the cottage occupied, and the fires lit to drive away the damp. The cottage was damp. Joel could pay for his keep by warming it well. He lit fires in all the rooms. He took down the filthy curtains and washed them. He had always had to do his own washing at Freda's stables, and wash the heavy horse blankets too.

He whitewashed the outside of the cottage; he found secondhand flagstones in a builder's yard and laid a paved path to what he discovered was called by his neighbours the Ty Bach, the little house. He

90

discovered that water came from a small spring in the wall that was piped into a pool where ducks swam. The water from the pipe was bright and clean and tasted wonderful.

Torr arrived on a grey day just before Christmas. He came alone, and he was in a black mood, which lightened a little as he looked at the clean room, and the bright fire, and the meal laid on the table. Joel laid a second place. He had bought newmade bread from the bakehouse, and there was farm butter and farm cheese; pickles and pickled onions, all of which were on sale in the post office, made by local farmers' wives who found this a useful way to make extra pennies.

'If you've a girl coming, I'll find somewhere else to go,' Joel said.

'I had a girl; she wasn't walking here; she got the horrors when she saw how remote the place is, and took the next train back. Like a fool, I told her we only have oil lamps and then she asked about the bathroom! Brought up too fancy, that young lady was.'

Joel suddenly wondered how she would have reacted if she had come here and he had never come to the place; and she had found dirty crockery and filthy bedding, and the stained table upstairs with the two cups that were a squalid reminder of another girl who had slept here before.

'You've made yourself comfortable,' Torr said.

'I offered to pay rent.'

'Oh, don't be so daft. I wasn't criticising. I hate this place. If you like, you can rent it; what girl wants to come out to this hole anyway?'

'You pick the wrong girls,' Joel said.

'What choice have I? The kind that would maybe make something of this would never come here for a weekend anyway; and I'm not the marrying kind.

Love 'em and leave 'em, that's me.'

'The marrying kind might be a better bet,' Joel said. Marrying wasn't in his book either, but nor were the casual encounters that Torr favoured; the girls Torr went out with never appealed to Joel.

'I'd like to rent,' Joel said. 'So long as I have a free hand; I could do things with this place.'

He had been there nearly six weeks. He enjoyed the freedom to do as he chose; the chance to adapt his work hours to suit himself, so that he might walk for hours over the hills, and then return and spend half the night cleaning the cottage, or painting a room. He had decorated the kitchen, whose walls were now a creamy white, the table and chairs scrubbed to reveal that they were made of pine; they were now polished; a ragrug, bought at a jumble sale, lay on the stone-flagged floor; the oak dresser, a beautiful piece of furniture, gleamed and held a willow pattern service that Joel had found in a box in the cupboard under the stairs. The blue and white patterned plates, upright on the ledges, reflected the firelight.

'That was my grandmother's wedding present,' Torr said. 'She was housekeeper up at the big house, and they gave her that when she married. She married the coachman, who worked for them till he died. When he died, they gave her the cottage. It was a small farm, long ago. Grandmother had saved her money all her life and she bought the three fields; they're rented out now for grazing, but if you want them back, the rent has to be renegotiated every year.

'What rent do you want?' Joel asked.

'Ten pounds a year; you pay all expenses, and keep it in repair. You'll not see me here again for dust, I can tell you. I'd stay for Christmas, but I've some rides; could do with a few winners again. I've been unlucky.'

That didn't sound like Torr. He had always ridden

well and ridden to win. Torr was changing. Maybe he was changing too, Joel thought. He had begun to make plans. He could see a way of making a living; maybe not a good way as yet, but it had a future, and maybe with the future would come enough money to realise his dream. He would transfer his savings to a local bank; use half to finance himself and save half, and save every penny he could.

'We'll go to a solicitor and get an agreement drawn up,' Joel said.

'What on earth for? Between friends, isn't it?'

'Suppose something happens that ends our friendship? I don't want to take this on and be out on my ear on a whim, because you've decided to get married,' Joel said.

'How do I race from here? Don't be daft, man. What do I want with this crummy dump? It's been nothing but a headache since I inherited it.'

'Why didn't you sell it? Or rent it?'

Torr grinned.

'It got the girls here and was somewhere to go. But girls talk, don't they? And once the news had got around most of the girls seemed to know what the place was like. This last one, she was from another area, but she wanted the bright lights, not a cottage in the country and no mod cons. No piped water, she said. Well, there is a pipe, I told her. It leads to the duck pond. We bath there. She didn't think it funny.'

Joel found himself wondering what the girls had said about the plank above the stream. He couldn't imagine any of Torr's companions taking that in their stride. He was glad when Torr left, two days later, after visiting the nearest town where a solicitor drew up an agreement for a ten-year lease.

Now he could put some of his dreams into action. The stables were cleaned out, and ready for use. The two end outhouses proved to have once housed chickens and they could house chickens again. He would have his own eggs; and his own meat. The pigsty would soon have a new occupant and he would grow his own bacon. He could take on orphan lambs.

Maybe start a herd.

It was good sheep country. He could buy pony mares and breed them. Children loved ponies. He might even show them; make a name for himself somehow. Make money for himself somehow. He needed to make a start.

He went down to the post office, where old Mr Savage greeted him with a smile.

'What are you having for your Christmas dinner, or are you going home?' he asked.

'I haven't a home,' Joel said. 'I'm not bothering with Christmas.'

'I wish you a merry Christmas,' yelled the parrot, and clambered round his cage, hanging upside down from the roof to glare at Joel with bright beady eyes. He let go, and landed on his perch and shook himself so that feathers flew.

'Dirty bird. Disgusting bird,' he said, in a high woman's voice, with a Welsh accent, and the old man laughed. 'That's Mrs Owen the hens,' he said. 'She hates that bird, and it will mimic her. She's afraid of psittacosis.'

Joel laughed. He enjoyed his visits to the post office. It was the only time that he had any conversation at all, and the postmaster had a sense of humour that appealed to Joel.

'Can't have you spending the day alone,' the old man said. 'I spend the day alone, but I do celebrate. Join me, and save an old man from solitude. I'll feed you right royally, I promise. I'm a very good cook. I used to be a chef in one of the big London hotels. Then when I married, we came here; it was a good life while my wife was alive. It's a bit bleak at times now. You'd be doing me a favour. It's not good to be alone at Christmas time.'

Christmas had not been fun since his grandfather died. Freda had given them a good meal; but work at the stables had to go on. Nobody could leave the horses ungroomed and unfed, or the stables dirty; or the mares about to foal on their own. There was little in the way of celebration there. Christmases when he was small had been spent with the mother's help who gloried in the name, quite undeserved, of Nanny. There had been little celebration, and he had only been there to eat the vast meal twice that he could remember. His father always gave him a Dickens book.

Nanny had always tried to see that he did enjoy the day and that it held the magic that all small children love. He remembered her with far more affection than he did his parents.

Grandfather had given him Sharina for Christmas. He had never spent such an exciting day. The mare had arrived the night before, when he was in bed. He heard the hoofbeats, as she walked across the yard. He peeped from the window and fell in love. He had never seen such a beautiful animal. He had no idea she was for him.

Next morning there had been garlands in the yard; they were laid on the ground, outlining a pathway leading to the stable, which was decorated with a holly wreath bright with berries and red ribbons. The mare had worn a tinsel halter, with a large label on it saying 'Happy Christmas, Joel.'

He had stood with tears of happiness pouring down his face, unable even to speak. Grandfather had left him with his mare, and sat at the table, where his other present waited for him. He couldn't even remember what they were. Joel had rushed in and enveloped the old man in a bear hug.

'Steady on, young man. I need to breathe,' Grandfather had said, laughing his big belly laugh, shaking all over, delighted with the reception of his gift.

It hurt to remember.

'I'd like to join you,' Joel said, coming back to the present. The memory had been so vivid that he was startled to find himself standing at the mahogany counter, the smell of cheese and soap and fresh-ground coffee in his nostrils. There were butterpats with cows on them, and the paired wooden patters lay clean and ready for a new customer.

The memory had been too vivid. He had almost smelled the warm stable and the rich scent of his new mare; and heard the rustle of straw as she moved.

'I would like to join you,' he said again.

'Good. I'll expect you at twelve in time for a glass of sherry. My wife and I always had a glass of sherry before Christmas dinner. Now, why did you come?'

'God rest you, merry gentlemen,' the parrot said.

Joel stood, wondering just why he had come. He wished he hadn't remembered Sharina.

'Hens,' he said. 'I'm renting the cottage. Where can I buy hens?'

'From my parrot's old enemy,' the postmaster said. 'She lives at the second cottage on the left down the lane. That'll be an education for you. Time you met her if you're going to live here. Be careful. The children say she's a witch.'

'What do you say?' Joel asked.

'I say that everyone needs to make up his own mind. She raises excellent hens. Just watch your step and don't mention parrots to her.'

'Poor Susie's lonely. Tom's dead,' the parrot said, and Joel went out of the shop thinking that life often seemed just as irrational as the bird itself.

CHAPTER 11

Mrs Owen's cottage was tiny; two rooms and a
kitchen, where she lived with six cats and an irritable
Jack Russell terrier who snarled at Joel as he came in
through the garden gate. A giant ginger Tom stalked
towards Joel, turned his back, arched it, and directed
a spray against the gatepost. A large white cockerel
strutted into the garden when the door was opened in
answer to Joel's knock.

The garden was winter dreary, but still held
memories of high summer: there were glistening
heads of honesty; a few moss roses hanging on to leaf-
less bushes, petals browning with rain; lupin seeds;
and the memories of summer hydrangeas were dotted
through the two big patches of ground on either side
of the gate. The ground was turned and weedless in
between the plants.

The stench of tomcat from the house caught in Joel's
nostrils so that he stepped backwards. The door had
been opened by a tiny woman, wearing a long black
dress that dragged on the floor; over it she wore a
purple cardigan, buttoned high, but buttoned
wrongly, and on top of that a dingy plaid shawl, long
worn into holes, but clutched tightly round her by
dirty wrinkled hands with blackened nails. Her small
brown face was dark as hazelnut, with eyes that
almost matched the skin. Joel guessed she had gypsy
ancestry.

'What do you want?' she asked, suspicion in her

voice. 'You're the young man that's borrowed Jim Torr's place. His son never was any good, to him or anyone else.'

Joel wondered what the village gossips said about him.

'I'm leasing it for the next ten years. Mr Savage says you have hens for sale.'

'Dead or alive?'

'I want them for laying,' Joel said.

'And what do you know about God's creatures, young man? Will you talk to them and gentle them, and soothe them when they're broody; and take their eggs kindly, and never harm them?'

'My grandfather had chickens on his farm. I used to help with them,' Joel said.

'And where is the old man now?'

'He died three years ago.'

He died three centuries ago, he died a lifetime ago, Joel thought bleakly. Nothing would ever be the same again.

'I've four young pullets soon to come into lay. Myfanwy and Rhiannon; Angharad and Eirwen. Treat them well, and they'll repay you a thousand-fold. Treat them badly and my curses will haunt you for ever and you'll lie and rot where the Hounds of Hades yell to the skies and hunt the wicked into early graves.'

'Grandfather used to speak of the Hounds of Hades,' Joel said.

'Then he was a wise man and he had the gift, and knew of hidden things,' the old woman said. She glared at him from under immense hairy eyebrows. The grey hairs of a thin moustache bristled on her upper lip.

'I don't tell the future except to a few, and then for silver, but I'll tell you about yourself, as the grandson of a Wise One. You've known a great loss; and a great sorrow. You've lost all hope, but it will return. You've lost a man you loved and a man you hated; and you harbour hatred, which will bring the Hounds on your heels. Forget bitterness and brooding. You're young. Start again. Follow the way and follow the only way; the way that will lead you into the light, and silence the baying Hounds for ever. Take my birds and take care of them. And watch John Savage the post; he is a frivolous man and commits a great evil, as he keeps a bird of the devil. He will catch a disease from it, and sicken and die.'

Joel stared at her.

'I'll bring the pullets.'

She turned and went inside, closing the doors behind her, shutting in the stench. Joel glanced through the window, into a tiny room, where firelight glowed on the walls, and on hundreds of tiny ornaments, animals of all kinds, crudely made, as if the old lady herself was the shaper. They were garishly painted and stood or lay or sat on high shelves round the top of the walls.

There were cushions on the floor and on every cushion lay a cat. One big tortoiseshell was sprawled on the hearthrug with kittens sucking from her.

There were flower patterns on the carpet, on the wallpaper, on the chair coverings, and flower paintings on the walls. The curtains were flowered. Joel thought he had never seen such a conflicting jazz of colour in any room in his life. It made his head ache to look.

The hen woman returned, carrying a big cardboard box tied with string.

'You have food and straw for them, and a warm place to lie?'

Joel had straw and a warm place to lie. He needed to

buy food, but today he could get it from the farmer across the fields. He wanted to get away from the cottage. He paid a pound for the pullets, sure that was over the price in the village, but not able to haggle.

'I'll take care of them,' he said.

'You have no choice. You will have a long life, and a chequered life. You will get what you want, many years in the future, by a path that will seem strange to you. And yet it will not be what you want at all. Your dearest wish will come true, and may come true soon; but again it will not be the way you want it. There are many obstacles in your life, but you will overcome them; and the Hounds of Hades will be with you forever, often baying at your heels. It will be many years before they leave you in peace.'

Joel, bemused by the spate of words, took the box and thanked her. She watched him walk down the path towards the rickety gate, her eyes staring. It was dusk and the grass verge at the lane edge was crisp with frost. He looked back to see her outlined by light from the window behind her; a tiny black figure, frightening in the intensity of her gaze. The ginger Tom was weaving round her legs, pushing against her, rubbing his head against her, adoring her.

As Joel glanced back, she opened the door and went inside, followed by the cat and the cockerel.

Walking back to his own cottage, he was unable to forget her words. The whole episode had seemed ridiculous, and yet it had an undercurrent of something that he could not identify. He did recognise, as he walked up the hill, that he was afraid of the old lady, and hoped, very hard, that her words were nonsense. He was not sure that they were.

He fetched the lamp from the cottage and took the hens into the henhouse. They had a good big indoor place, nesting boxes, and a large outdoor run, made as safe as he could make it against foxes. He needed a cat to keep the mice and rats down. Maybe he could have one of the old lady's kittens, although he didn't much want to encounter her again.

The hens were pretty; red speckled creatures that fled from the box into a remote corner of the henhouse and stared at him, their beady eyes reminding him of old Mrs Owen's eyes. It had begun to rain heavily and the thought of walking across the fields in the dark did not appeal to him. He cut several slices of brown bread and threw it down for them, but they made no move to eat it. It would take time for them to settle.

He cooked himself a piece of haddock he had bought from the post office; the fish man came every Friday.

Then he settled by the fire, a notebook in front of him. Grandfather had taught him to keep accounts; to write down every penny; to write down his plans.

'Once it's on paper, boy, it's harder to forget,' the old man said.

He needed to grow his own food; buy nothing, to save money. Maybe later he could sell eggs and chickens; maybe he could grow enough surplus to sell to his neighbours; he intended to go to the beast sale and see if he could pick up a pony; it would be good to have a horse to care for again. A mare in foal would be best; if he could afford her. He could sell the foal.

He was spending money; on paint and on wood, even though that was second-hand, from old demolished houses. On food and on a pair of good strong boots. He could grow nothing till summer. The hard work had eased his anger; the feeling of being his own man was bringing back a desire to work and to work for the future. He had put his own mark on the cottage and sold some of Torr's furniture, with Torr's permission, and sent on the money to Newmarket.

He had bought himself a second-hand easy chair at an auction sale and two chests for the bedroom. A large black sheepskin rug, bought from the local butcher, was pure extravagance, but it gave the room a luxurious appearance.

Joel was surprising himself by his need for comfort.

He walked across the fields next day to Craig yr Afon, the farmhouse that he could see from his kitchen window. It was an odd building, consisting downstairs of one huge room and a minute kitchen, and upstairs also of one room only. The cobbled yard was spotless, in spite of the massed cattle that grazed in the field beyond it. A man came from the milking parlour. He was little older than Joel, big built, with fair hair that grew thick and wavy, and needed cutting; he had soft blue eyes and a ready smile.

'I hear you've taken a lease on Llain Grin,' he said.

Joel nodded.

'I need chicken feed; would you have any to spare that I can buy? I bought four pullets yesterday from Mrs Owen the Hens.'

'You are in favour. She doesn't sell to everybody. Did she tell your future?'

'After a fashion,' Joel said. 'It was odd; and not exactly promising.'

'She's a nasty knack of hitting on the truth,' the man said. 'I'm Arfon Griffiths. My dad farmed here and now it's mine. The old man died last year, after a fall from his horse out hunting. Old Mrs Owen warned him, after a fashion. Said he'd come to a violent end through something he loved too much; and he did fair worship that mare, but she could be wicked. Come in for a drink, and meet my wife.'

Joel had expected a country girl. Instead he found himself facing a slender wisp of a woman, wearing unexpectedly rich material, her dress in the latest fashion, he guessed, as it was a style new to him and not worn by the other village women. Her dark hair was cut close against her head, framing a milky skin, and she smiled at him, a welcome shining from enormous eyes that reminded him of Sharina's eyes; dark, lustrous and long-lashed. She was beautiful.

She spoke very little, and when she moved he realised that she was pregnant; the outline of the child was just beginning to show. Her voice was soft, a slow drawl, and she was as English as he was.

She poured tea and passed round a plate of hot home-made scones, and went out of the room.

'Annette's lost here,' Arfon said. 'She's not used to farming, or to such a lonely place, and she doesn't really have enough to fill her time, although she makes her own clothes and she does a bit of writing. I hope the baby will make a difference. Come over and see us; she needs extra company.'

But not my company, Joel thought, as he walked back along the footpath, shouldering a sack of chicken feed that he was sure had been sold to him far too cheaply. He had liked Arfon and would like to see more of him.

That night he dreamed of Sharina and as he went to halter her, she turned into a slender dark-haired woman with lustrous eyes who laughed at him and invited him, holding out her arms. He woke, breathing as if he had been running and knew that it would not be wise to visit his neighbour too often.

By Christmas the pullets had settled in. He kept the hen lady's names for them, although he had no idea which was which. It didn't seem to matter. They came running together when he put out their grain. He could soon tell one from another, and gave each the name he thought fitted.

Myfanwy was greedy and bossy and chivvied the

others away from her when she fed. Rhiannon was timid, always last and always losing her share, so that he took her out after the first week and fed her on her own in the other henhouse.

Eirwen was a persistent clucker, always vocal, as if exclaiming continuously on life. Angharad was the first always to come when he called the hens; but she deferred to Myfanwy, waiting patiently until the more aggressive bird had taken the edge from her appetite and would allow the others to share.

They amused Joel. They were the first of his stock, the forerunners of the future, and the first living things he had owned apart from Sharina. One day, about a week after he had bought them, he went out into the yard and found old Mrs Owen standing by the run, looking at them.

'You'll do,' she said, and walked off again, her long dress trailing in the mud. Joel thought he could smell cat long after she'd gone.

The next morning he found two eggs in the nesting boxes, and that afternoon he came home from a walk to discover a cardboard box on the front doorstep. Something inside it moved. He took it indoors and opened it, to stare into the eyes of a tawny kitten, sitting bolt upright and indignant. It sat on a crocheted square of blanket and, in a section of the box, partitioned off, was a small tin in which was a parcel containing cooked fish. There was also a scrawled note in large childish handwriting.

'Here is the kitten you wanted. Take care of her. Her mother is a good mowser. She likes goats' milk. Get a goat. It will keep the grass down and you can have milk and cheese. Don't let her out yet and butter her paws.'

Joel, looking at the note, decided Mrs Owen was definitely a witch. Nobody knew he needed a cat. It was not until he was drifting off to sleep that night that he remembered he had bought a mousetrap. It only needed Mr Savage to tell the old lady, and she would put two and two together as fast as the next person. It was certainly a way of getting rid of a kitten. From what he had seen of the village houses, nearly everybody had one cat already and the females always seemed to be pregnant.

He laughed at himself. Living alone was addling his wits.

He could not maintain his anger. He was too busy, and for the first time in his life he had a challenge to meet. His four years with Freda had been free-wheeling years, learning years, during which he planned a future that, with the money from the selling of the farm, would have been easy to fulfill.

He still intended to have his own stud farm; but that would now be far in the future, and he would have to earn his own money, every step of the way.

There were black days when the fury returned; and there were days when he fed the hens and put the kitten in an outhouse with food and a box of earth and walked until he was exhausted. Those were the days when Annette Griffiths called in with a gift of scones or cake, knowing he lived alone and had no one to bake for him. He was so disturbed by her visits that he wished she wouldn't come, but to tell her so would have been churlish. He did not know how to treat her, and she laughed at him when he stammered or blushed, and told Arfon their new neighbour was shy.

On Christmas Eve Arfon and Annette came together, bringing a holly wreath and an iced Christmas cake, mince pies and a wrapped gift tied with ribbon. Joel, who hadn't thought of buying them anything, was embarrassed, and found it difficult to voice his thanks.

'I've nothing for you,' he said.

'Oh, but you have,' Annette said. 'We haven't nearly enough holly and the three trees behind your house are full of berries; and there's mistletoe on the oak. We stole it last year; we can't do that now!'

Joel and Arfon took the lamps and went out to cut the berried branches. When they returned the table was spread with a vivid cloth, the edge festooned with garlands of berried holly and scarlet ribbons in long embroidered trails. The table was laid for three; a cold chicken and a potato salad; mince pies, and sausage rolls; a bottle of wine and two glasses.

'It isn't good for babies if their mothers drink,' Annette said laughing. 'I'm going to have the health-iest baby in the world.'

Joel watched her. He had never seen any woman so beautiful. Grandfather's words came back to him, a lesson long learned in childhood. Thou shalt not covet thy neighbour's goods; nor his wife, or his ox, or his ass ... Joel had forgotten how it went. If only he had met her long ago; but what would he have had to offer her?

A promise of fairy gold that vanished before he could touch it; three years of dreams that had been blown away by the chill wind of reality. It was as well he hadn't met any girl who took his fancy.

His neighbours put his silence down to shyness.

'We go over to friends for Christmas Day,' Annette said. 'And to Arfon's school chum for Boxing Day. Will you be alone?'

'Mr Savage invited me,' Joel said.

They did not tell him that Mr Savage always invited at least one lonely villager to share his Christmas food.

'He has been very lonely since his wife died. It must be six years ago now,' Annette said.

'Next Christmas they'll all have to come to us. I'm not lugging a baby across those fields on a winter night,' Annette said, some time later, sitting on the sheepskin rug, gazing into the fire. 'I wonder what our haunt will do when the baby's born.'

'Haunt?' Joel said.

'What did the farmhouse smell of when you came in?' Arfon asked.

'Lilac,' Joel said. He had been struck by the overwhelming scent, out of season, unexpected, and thought that Annette must have been wearing perfume.

His visitors laughed.

'It liked you,' Annette said.

'Joel thinks we're mad.' Arfon lifted his glass and looked into its yellow depths. 'The farmhouse is haunted by something that fills it with fragrance. Everyone seems to smell something different. Annette smells lavender; I smell ripe apples and cooking bacon; our cowman swears he smells sage and onion stuffing all the time he is indoors and the vicar smells incense, which he doesn't like so he suspects us of heretical practices. I can't think why it should produce that scent for him!'

'Maybe I produce an odd effect on him, and his thoughts produce the perfume he associates with me,' Annette said.

Joel looked at her, and had a vision of her standing watching him with grave eyes, her arms filled with branches of white lilac. There had been a white lilac tree in Grandfather's garden.

He didn't know whether he was sorry or glad when the evening ended, and he watched the lights of their handlamps bobbing as they walked back along the footpath through the dark, their voices and laughter carrying to him on the wind.

108

He went indoors, and the kitten clambered onto his lap, a small purring bundle, and curled against him. He sat, staring into the fire, knowing that the Hounds were baying tonight. It was a long time before he summoned the energy to wash up. Annette's gift lay on the table. She had cleared away and stacked the dishes and folded the cloth and taken it with her, but had left the remains of the food, and another bottle of wine. The small parcel lay beside it, with a card in an envelope.

Joel put the card on the dresser. It was the only card he was likely to get. Nobody but Torr knew his address, and Torr wasn't likely to remember him. He looked at the picture; of coaches in the snow and women in Victorian dresses.

He opened the parcel. Annette had knitted him a woollen cap. It would keep his ears warm when he went about the winter's outdoor jobs and he would treasure it. It was good to have neighbours who thought about him, but he did wish this neighbour didn't have such a beautiful wife.

He wore the cap when he walked down to the village post office next day.

Christmas dinner, surprisingly, consisted of jugged hare, with vegetables in a delicious sauce, followed by a trifle into which most of the sherry bottle seemed to have been tipped. Susie punctuated the meal with odd remarks and once burst into loud song.

'Once in Royal David's city . . .'

'There's a card for you. Thought I'd save it to give you today,' the postmaster said.

Joel was sitting, relaxed, and pleasantly dreamy, looking into the fire. He had brought six eggs as a present. They were still a luxury as the hens weren't yet in full lay. He opened the card, wondering that Torr had bothered.

It was from Freda.

'I got your address from Torr. Sharina's stable is for sale; he lost his money in the crash. Every horse in the place has to go. Hope you are well. We are busy. Thought you'd like to know.'

Joel looked at the words.

He wished that Freda hadn't told him. He could no more buy Sharina now than he could make a million pounds on the Stock Exchange, but he knew he had to try to get her back. It was the opportunity he had been waiting for.

The postmaster, good at reading expressions, asked no questions, but filled Joel's glass again. They were drinking a potent home-made elderberry wine and by teatime they were singing with the parrot, singing Christmas carols, and laughing at tales of the village and its past inhabitants.

'I've been here now for over twenty years,' the old man said. 'When I first came one of my miseries was old Jones the Goats. He was simple, and slept with his goats and stank like his goats. He emptied the post office in minutes when he came.' The old man refilled both glasses and sighed. 'He's been dead for over sixteen years. Time goes. Then there was old Mrs Owen's grandmother; she was a tartar and if she didn't like the cheese she would come back to the shop and grab my hair and rub it in my face.'

The parrot cackled suddenly as if she had understood. She gripped a bar of her cage in her beak as if trying to bite through it and then shook herself, feathers flying.

'Dirty bird!' she said, in Mrs Owen's voice.

Joel left the post office at eight o'clock, and walked, a little unsteadily, back up the frosty lane. As the cold air cleared his head he remembered Freda's card, and he wondered again how he could get Sharina back.

110

He began to despair that she would ever be his again.

The kitten, released from the outhouse, greeted him ardently, anticipating food, and followed him up the path to the front door. There was a cardboard box on the step. He stooped to pick it up, and something inside rustled.

He took it indoors, and, opening it cautiously, saw the red comb and bright eyes of a young cock. He took him outside and put him in the spare henhouse.

Inside the box was a note.

'You need this. His names Gwyn. Happy Crismas. Eleri Owen.'

He laughed at her spelling.

It was the oddest Christmas Joel had ever spent.

CHAPTER 12

There was no time for brooding when winter hardened its grip. Joel added a goat to his ménage, and milked her, and took the milk to Annette who made it into cheese for him. He bought a young mare at the beast sale. She was cheap because she had spiteful ways, but he soon discovered she owed those to mismanagement. Later he would breed from her. Meanwhile, he bought a fifth-hand saddle and bridle, and rode her. She responded quickly to kindness. She had known little of that, he was sure.

She was farm-bred and kept rough, and nobody had bothered with her. He thought her shapely, and she had all the assets his grandfather had demanded of a good brood mare. He stabled her. At first she was afraid of the dark stall, but soon she took it for granted, and spent the nights warm, instead of standing out in all weathers and grazing hard ground in the bitter winter frosts.

She hated grooming; nobody had ever bothered about that either, and her mane and tail were a dirty tangled mess. The first time Joel tried to wash her tail in suds in a bucket she landed a kick that lamed him for a week. He could not bear to see her unkempt. His training at Freda's had ensured that his horses would always be immaculate.

February brought day after day of heavy rain. The brook became a raging torrent, surging, peaty brown, over its banks. The lower field was a lake of steel-grey water, lying bleak under a sodden sky. Ducks and gulls floated on the surface. Wintry trees fretted the horizon, and often the wind screamed down the valley and tore around the house, sending the kitten crazy so that it leaped after anything that moved, and chased its tail in frenzy.

There was never enough daylight. Water had to be fetched, and often the ice had to be broken, although the pipe never froze. There was wood to chop and the hens to feed and the goat to milk and the mare to care for. He delighted in the familiar chores, even in mucking out her stable, and laying fresh straw, and leading her in, to nose at her haynet, and rub her head against his arm. He was at ease with horses as he never was with people.

Arfon looked after his beasts for him while he took two days off to go to the auction sale. He wanted to know who bought Sharina. She was sold for five hundred pounds to a man he disliked on sight. A big man, his clothes tight on a body that seemed to strain out of them, the muscles run to fat, the face, with its heavy jowls and cold eyes and thick fleshy lips, the face of a selfish man with no thought for others. His black wavy hair lay thickly plastered against his head. The groom who led Sharina out dodged as he passed him, as if afraid of a kick and Joel went home sickened at the thought of his mare in such hands.

There was nothing he could do.

He met old Mrs Owen on his way back to the cottage.

'The Hounds are baying tonight,' she said.

That night the wind blew with such force that he thought he could really hear the Hounds baying, surrounding him, mocking him, hunting him, driving him. He needed money for Sharina. Money. Money. How did a man earn money in a hurry? It couldn't be done, or not legally. Or could it be done? He lay awake, tossing restlessly, listening to the scream of the gale and the rain that drove against the windows, and turned over one idea after another in his brain.

The wind died, and snow came. The snow lay for a week, and he helped men find their sheep; every male in the village turned out to rescue the beasts. The snow thawed and then came a week of hard frosts, with the yard icy, so that Joel put socks over his boots to try and keep his footing, and dared not move the mare lest she fell and broke a leg.

There was no time to visit or be visited, so that he was startled one evening by a thunderous knock on the door. The kitten, which had been sitting on his lap, bolted under the dresser, staring out at him with frightened eyes.

Joel opened to find Arfon standing outside, his face grey with misery.

'Joel, for God's sake, can you go for the doctor? Annette's fallen on the ice; she's losing the baby . . . I must get back.'

He was gone again, and Joel grabbed his outdoor clothes and the cap that Annette had knitted, took the handlamp, and went out into the dark. He had no idea where the doctor lived, but the postmaster would know. If the doctor lived in the village it would be far quicker for him to reach the farm by the footpath than to drive the six miles down the narrow twisting lanes.

He hammered on the post office door.

He waited while old Mr Savage telephoned. He stared blindly at the parrot cage. Susie was hidden by a white cloth. All was silent, except for the postmaster's urgent voice.

'The doctor will pick you up. I told him about the footpath. He lives outside the village, and would have to drive through and round the lanes,' the old post-

114

master said. 'I was just having a last cup of tea.' He poured a second cup and Joel stood drinking it, watching the clock, urging the doctor to hurry, counting the speeding minutes. It seemed a year before he heard the grunting engine as the car laboured up the hill.

The doctor was grey-haired and brusque. He opened the passenger door and Joel jumped in, directing him to his own cottage. They stumbled together across the icy fields, along the rutted path, once stepping, both cursing, into water thinly covered by ice that wetted them to the ankles.

The farmhouse lights guided them.

Arfon stood at the door. His eyes stared at them blankly, and, after one look at him, the doctor ran into the house.

'The blood,' Arfon said. 'All the blood.'

Time stood still. The minutes seemed endless. Joel had nothing to say. The doctor appeared at last and looked at them.

'She would never have survived the birth, nor the child,' the doctor said. 'They would have bled to death together; there was a central placenta. That's what has happened now. I'm sorry.'

Arfon walked outside. The doctor looked after him.

'A one in a million chance,' he said unhappily. 'There's nothing can be done now. I'll send the nurse to lay her out. Can you stay with him?'

Joel nodded. He would have to guide the doctor back to the cottage and his car and then return. He moved like a man in a dream, unable to understand that Annette, who had been so alive, was now dead. He would have to guide the nurse too, he thought, but the doctor said that she knew the way well and was never afraid in the dark. She'd find the place by herself. Go back to Arfon.

Arfon was standing by the couch on which Annette had died. The doctor had covered her with a blanket. It was already stained with blood. Arfon had turned it back and was looking at the dead face.

'She'd just made supper,' he said. 'We never ate it.'

Joel went into the kitchen and made a fresh pot of tea. He had to do something. He poured it into two cups, and added milk and sugar. They sat, one each side of the fire, conscious of the dead woman behind them, watching the flames fade, and neither drank.

The nurse found them sitting in silence by the embers of the fire. She built the blaze up again.

'Take him home with you,' she said to Joel. 'I'll stay with her. I've work to do; I'm used to the dead. He can't stay here.'

Arfon followed Joel obediently, as if no longer able to think for himself. He walked where he was told to walk; he avoided the icy water when told; and he sat in the armchair, and huddled into it, holding the kitten as if it were a talisman against ill fortune. He began to shake; a violent uncontrollable shivering that went on and on. Joel filled a stone hot-water bottle and fetched blankets, and poured some of the wine that Annette had brought at Christmas.

It was nearly three in the morning when Joel managed to help the man up the stairs and put him to sleep in his bed. He went back to build the fire and sit, feeling sick himself, to nurse a grief he could never disclose to anyone.

That night he learned, in full, the meaning of his grandfather's words.

'If only . . . those are the saddest words in the whole world, lad.'

He dozed, and dreamed of a woman who stood with her arms full of white lilac blossom and laughed at him. He went towards her and she flung the

116

flowers in his face and ran, running through fields and woods, running into the distance; and when he woke his face was wet with tears.

He washed and shaved and fed the animals. When he returned Arfon was standing, dressed, in his sitting room.

'It's time to milk the cows,' he said.

Joel walked back with him, and they sat together in the milking parlour. Joel was conscious that he was using Annette's stool. Only yesterday she would have sat where he was sitting, doing her share of the chores. Milking was something she still could have done. It was some years since Joel had tried his hand at milking but the old skill came back.

There was solace of a kind in routine; in putting the milk into churns; in taking the churns to the lane and putting them on the table that stood there to make it easier for the lorry driver; in cleaning the milking parlour and washing down the yard.

They were late and the lorry came as they lifted the last churn.

'I'm sorry, Arfon, it's too bad,' the man said, awkwardly, feeling he ought to say something. The news had been spread by the nurse.

Arfon looked at him as if he hadn't heard and went back to let the cattle into the field.

'It's bloody bad luck,' the man said. 'There's no words . . .' He drove away, leaving Joel looking after him, wondering how they would get through the next few days. He felt completely out of his depth, unable to cope. He went indoors; they would have to eat, but they couldn't eat here, with Annette lying in the downstairs room, and there was no room to sit in the kitchen.

He cut thick chunks of bread, found butter and cheese, feeling like an intruder as he hunted through

117

the cupboards. He put water in the kettle to boil. Arfon had piped water.

Joel took cups and sandwiches outside, and they ate in the yard, looking over the gate at the cattle. Arfon was still moving like a man in a daze, doing the familiar chores and also doing everything Joel told him. He ate, and he drank, but he said nothing. One of the cows moved up to the gate and put her head through to be stroked; she was a pretty gentle animal, their only Jersey cow, kept for her rich milk and cream and had been Annette's favourite, almost a pet. Arfon stood stroking her, as if contact with her might bring his wife back to him.

Joel went round the farm and did the necessary chores, caring for the pigs and the chickens and the two goats. Both needed milking. Annette preferred goats' milk for their own consumption.

People began to call. Arfon listened to them and thanked them for coming, and Joel made tea and offered cakes; the cake tins were all full. The room smelled of summer hayfields; the scent of lilac was gone.

Arfon, later, swore that the room, for all of those weeks after Annette had died, smelled of hyacinths; sweet, overpowering and sickly.

Annette lay coffined and the women came to see her. Joel had gone to look at her, to say his last goodbye. The white face with its cap of dark hair was serene. He stared down at her, and then, with a shock of disbelief, saw the face of the child, cradled against her dead cheek. He had forgotten the child.

He blundered out of the room, and ran for home, twice falling, lying where he fell and hammering the hard earth, in a frenzy of misery. He could not face the house; he went to his childhood refuge, the quiet stable where he lay in the straw, and choked himself

118

with harsh sobs that he couldn't stop. The mare nosed him, as Sharina once had comforted him when young and consoled him for some childhood error for which he had been punished.

He lay in the straw, hating God, who had visited this cruelty on them.

The village women helped with the funeral; they baked and they brewed and they brought Arfon scones and pies and pasties; to call to talk to him. Joel called too, but Arfon did not want anyone. He wanted to be alone; to work on the farm, and to sit alone, brooding. Joel became afraid that he might take his own life and one morning, after Arfon had gone with the cattle to the far field, he took all the ammunition from the house and made sure that the gun was not loaded.

One morning, about six weeks after the funeral, he went out into his yard to find old Mrs Owen once more inspecting his hens. The cock was now with them. She looked at him.

'Now the Hounds are baying for two of you,' she said. 'A wife; a love; and one that can never be told.'

Joel stared at her.

'Don't worry. I tell no one what the spirits tell me; I know many secrets. They can't be hidden from a Wise One. Your grandfather must have known secrets too.'

'Only horse secrets,' Joel said.

She cackled, suddenly and unexpectedly, and Joel realised where the parrot had learned to make such an odd sound.

'Seven years' bad luck and then fortune changes,' she said. 'Arfon Griffiths is just starting his, but he has had what you will never have. You have had four years of your ill time already. Three more years of service. Seven for him. He'll go away; and there will be changes affecting you. But not yet. There's still time to serve.'

She turned and walked away. As she opened the gate she looked towards him, and, quite unnervingly, smiled. He had never seen her smile before.

'Life's like a see-saw,' she said. 'Up and down; up and down. I've known it all and seen it all. I'm nearly eighty now; and my time remaining is short. It's sad to die young; wasting, it seems. But there's a reason; a meaning; a teaching; for both of you; it was time for her. She'd done what she was put on earth to do. You'll know that one day. Maybe not till you reach my age.'

The gate swung to behind her and the goat bleated. Joel watched until her small odd figure was out of sight. He went indoors, feeling as he always did after an encounter with her, that reason had flown and life become totally irrational.

It was time to go across and help Arfon with the milking.

He went daily and they shared the chores between them. Arfon said little. They worked in silence most of the time. Joel wondered if he were wanted or needed, but he could not leave the man alone. At night he looked from his room across the fields and saw lights burning, nightlong, never turned out.

Arfon looked like a ghost man; he had lost weight and had no will to go on. Morning revealed the dirty glass and the empty bottles. Joel washed up and tidied and made food that was rarely eaten and said nothing.

The day after Mrs Owen's visit Arfon spoke, in the middle of milking.

'I'm selling up. I can't go on here. Not when the daffodils come. She planted daffodils everywhere this year; for the baby to see flowers. She loved flowers.'

Joel had seen the daffodil spikes. They grew in the

120

hedge banks, they grew in the grassy patch Annette had called a lawn; they grew in the orchard, under the fruit trees; they grew along the edge of the lane outside the gate.

'Would you like to buy the place? You could run both easily in tandem. This house is warmer and better found than the cottage; and the mare would do better in my good stables.'

'I couldn't afford it,' Joel said. He wished he could; he could make something of this place, even with its memories.

'Pay what you have, and the rest as it comes. I don't want the place; I don't want the bother of selling; I just want to get away. I've nobody now. I was an only child and my parents are both dead. Annette grew up in an orphanage. I'd rather you had it than anyone. It would make up, perhaps, for what you lost.'

'What I lost?'

'Your grandfather's farm; and the lost money.'

'How did you know about that?' Joel was sure he had told nobody.

'You told Mr Savage at Christmas. You drank too much of his home-made wine; and told him about your grandfather, and your childhood, and your parents. And your mare. He didn't know it was a confidence. It didn't seem to matter, and he was sorry for you.'

Joel could remember little of the later part of his Christmas visit. He remembered, vaguely, stumbling back along the dark lane, and that was all. He had wakened with a vile head, and sworn not to sample the home-made heady stuff again.

'It doesn't really matter,' Joel said.

'I've made an appointment with my solicitor. I don't need much cash, not the way I'm going to live. I'll probably join the merchant navy. You can pay me

121

what you can afford, and pay the rest over the years. It doesn't matter to me.'

The offer was too tempting to resist. The farmhouse and the cattle; the stock; land of his own, instead of a leased property. A stake for the future, instead of the possibility that at the end of ten years Torr might change his mind and refuse to renew the lease.

They went together into the town, and Joel signed a contract to buy. He was to pay £200 down and the rest in instalments, and the first payment was to be made a month ahead.

He said goodbye to Arfon at the end of the week. His neighbour took little with him. A small case of clothes, and his gun.

Joel was on his own. He went round the farmhouse after milking. He wouldn't move in yet; he would keep the house aired and make changes. He would burn the settee on which Annette had died.

He was just about to leave when he heard the howling. He had forgotten Skip, Annette's dog. Since her death Skip had been kept outside, in one of the outhouses. He was a quiet beast, elderly now, half collie, half heaven-knew-what. Arfon had been unable to do anything but feed him. The dog had been Annette's shadow, and also the cause of her fall, running to greet her and tripping her up as he leaped at her on the icy ground.

Joel had not realised the animal was still there.

He opened the shed door and Skip crept out and lay at his feet, looking up at him. He had not seen daylight for weeks. Joel looked at the dog.

'Come on, then,' he said, and went indoors to find food, and watch the animal wolf it. He wondered if Arfon had always remembered to feed the poor brute. He left it free, wondering where it would settle. When he crossed the yard to climb the stile to the footpath and go home to feed his own stock, the dog followed. When he looked back, it went down, as if eyeing a sheep, and when he said nothing, it came after him, always yards behind.

He reached the cottage, and the dog crouched at the gate. As he looked at it, it wagged its tail, half-heartedly, as if unsure of its welcome.

'Come on, then,' Joel said, as he opened the front door. The dog raced inside, as if afraid he might change his mind. There was a flurried sound of racing paws, and an explosive hiss as the cat leaped for sanctuary on top of a cupboard. The dog stood beneath, looking up at the cat, which perched, back arched, fur fluffed, making it look enormous, swearing menacingly. Skip's tail was wagging, his ears were pricked, his head was tilted to one side, his eyes were bright and interested.

Grandfather had always had cats and dogs. Cat would just have to learn to put up with it. Joel realised he had never even given the cat a name. She was now threequarters grown, a handsome tawny, and doing her job well. Any mouse showing its face inside the house regretted it.

'Lie down, Skip,' Joel said. 'And you'll just have to learn, young Mowser.'

He remembered Mrs Owen's odd spelling, and for the first time for weeks, he laughed.

He went to see the solicitor on the first of March. The money was due and he had it with him. He left Skip shut in with the mare, as the dog seemed to have adopted her, and often went to visit her in her stable, and lie beside her in the straw. Joel took the train into the town.

The solicitor's office was reached by a few steps up from a yard behind a hairdresser's shop. It was a gloomy room, the only spot of brightness coming from a log fire that crackled in a small grate.

Richard Grant was a tall man, beak-nosed, surprisingly shock-headed, in contrast to his dapper dress. He would never see forty again. He was a daunting man, with a dour manner, that seemingly disapproved of everything humans could think of doing. To Joel's surprise, there was a police officer with him.

'I've brought the money,' Joel said.

'I think you should read this first.' Richard Grant handed him a letter.

Joel opened it, puzzled, and began to read the angular spiky writing.

Dear Joel,
I can't go on. When you get this I'll be dead. The farm's yours, and everything in it. Richard Grant has my will. There's no one to leave it to. There's not much money in the bank, but you'll remedy that. Don't grieve for me; I'll be where I want to be; with Annette and my son.
God be with you, as he was not with me.
Arfon

Joel stared at the letter, and read it again, and again. He stared at the two men, unable to speak. The solicitor stood up and went to a cupboard and took from it a bottle of brandy. He poured a small amount into a glass and handed it to Joel. The warmth of the spirit was comforting.

Joel looked at the policeman.

'How?' he asked, although he knew. He saw the defeated figure walking down the lane, the case in one hand, the gun in the other.

'He shot himself, sir,' the man said.

'I took away the ammunition.'

The man shrugged. He was a burly man, his hair

124

greying, his eyes looking as if he had seen too much sorrow.

'Did you expect him to kill himself then, sir?'

'At first, yes. Not now . . . I don't know . . . he was drinking heavily . . . he didn't seem able to forget . . .'

'We need formal identification, sir. And you'll be needed at the inquest, to give evidence on his frame of mind.'

Joel felt as if he would never laugh again.

That night, sitting at home in the armchair, with Mowser wary, perched on top of the cupboard, and the dog lying at his feet, its head on his shoe, grateful for warmth and company again, Joel could not settle. He made his supper and ate it, the plate on his knees, sharing the food with the dog. Hunger had left him. His mind ran the picture of Arfon, walking away down the lane, carrying the gun, over and over, and he could not think of anything else. When his thoughts did change track they brought him the memory of another dead face; a face he had not seen. He had had to go and look at Arfon. They had done their best but nothing could hide the shotgun wound. Had his father looked like that, Joel wondered, and where had he gone to shoot himself? Arfon had chosen a lonely field, and died at night under the unpitying stars. A farmer had found him. Who had found Joel's father? For the first time since his father's death, he felt something like pity for his mother.

The knock on the door was hesitant. He wondered who could be calling. Nobody ever visited him since Annette's death, except Mrs Owen, who appeared unable to leave her hens entirely to his care, and came to inspect them, arriving always, unnervingly, when he least expected her. He could not bear a visit now from the hen woman.

He opened the door.

The postmaster stood there, a bottle of wine in one hand.

'I thought you could do with some company,' the old man said. 'It doesn't do to be too much alone.'

'I'll be poor company,' Joel said.

'No poorer than Arfon must have been for you. What are neighbours for?'

Joel opened the door wide. The old man stepped inside, and removed his coat, hanging it on one of the hooks in the passage.

He uncorked the wine.

'One glass only,' Joel said. 'I hear I burdened you with my worries at Christmas.'

'Such tales are better shared than left to fester,' the postmaster said. He beamed at Joel, who felt a sudden stir of friendship that was almost affection for the small portly man with his gnomish face and grey moustache that dropped around his mouth.

'You heard then,' Joel said.

'You don't keep many secrets in a village, lad. Nobody is surprised. He worshipped her and so did many others. We all miss her. She was kind to everyone; she had laughter, and she cared. We all knew how much she was looking forward to her baby.'

He sighed.

'An inquest. And then a funeral. And then a few lines in the newspaper, and the end of two lives. I sat by my wife when she was dying . . . and that's a long time ago now . . . and wondered what there is to come for any of us. Justice? Reckoning? Warmth to welcome us, or a long cold lying in limbo, unknown, non-existent. Hey, this won't cheer either of us, lad. Stir the fire and pour another glass and let's chase the megrims away. We can do no good by sitting here mumping.'

126

Joel sat and sipped the wine, and listened to the keening wind that always, nowadays, sounded like hounds baying. Arfon's hounds had known victory and chased him down to hell. The wine was comforting, but he would never seek solace in a bottle as Arfon had done. His grandfather had taught him to face the pack that devilled him; never run away, lad. The old man's voice came back to him, from a past that seemed centuries away.

The dog at his feet whimpered in his sleep and his legs pounded, as if he too were running. Joel, looking down at him, wondered what he was dreaming.

The postmaster left soon after nine o'clock. There was a high moon riding, teased by vagrant clouds. Beyond it were the pinpricked stars. Joel listened to the receding footsteps and stood, looking at the sky. Skip, oblivious of anything beyond his own needs, ran to the gate and cocked a leg against the post.

The mare whinnied, asking for company. The moon vanished, hidden by the invaders. It would rain soon. The moon was a fortress; the clouds an intruding army, blotting out her light. Startled by his own fancy, Joel went to bid the mare goodnight, and whistle the dog from his investigations of the ground where, moments before, a weasel had run by. Mowser had gone out into the darkness, but, at Joel's call, came in and settled herself on the cupboard top. She no longer arched and spat and swore but it was still an uneasy truce.

Joel could not face sleep. He was sure that he would be tormented by nightmares; he knew that if he went to bed he would only lie there wishing the days past were back again, that he had done more for Arfon, had comforted him, tried harder to console him, to make him face the future and build a new life. Arfon's death was Joel's failure. Yet what could he have said

127

or done? How could he have penetrated that obsessive grief?

He stared into the flames, guilt-ridden, and saw again the white face and black hair; the brilliant eyes that had laughed at him; and then the living face was replaced by the dead face; with the child at her shoulder, cuddled close in death as he never had been in life.

The days passed, with a nightmare-like quality that never seemed to lift. Joel gave evidence at the inquest. He stumbled through the evidence, blaming himself, in his own mind, though nobody blamed him at all.

The words of the verdict remained in his thoughts for all the years to come. Suicide during a fit of temporary insanity.

Joel standing outside, staring at the traffic, was aware of the police sergeant he had met in the solicitor's office.

'I ought to have done more for him,' Joel said.

'Don't blame yourself, sir. None of us can do much for each other; you were there daily; you helped all you could; he was never your responsibility. Maybe it's best this way. It's hard to say. There are times when I can't make up my own mind about anything and I'm older than you.' He smiled, briefly, but the smile was not of amusement. 'Don't quote me, sir. It's not an opinion I'd care to have attached to my name. But the dead never suffer; only we who are left behind.'

He nodded and walked away.

The doctor who had come to Annette when she died came out of the hall.

'Can I give you a lift?' he asked.

Joel accepted gratefully.

'Grief does strange things to people,' the doctor said, navigating the traffic skilfully. 'Don't blame yourself. You will, but don't. Each of us is responsible for his own life; we live it alone; we die alone. Others may impinge on us briefly, but in the end, we are our own masters. We make our own fates; we forge our own hells.'

CHAPTER 13

It was February once more.

Snow threatened from a steely sky with a yellow glare behind it.

Joel had been out on the hill all day, bringing down the sheep which he had bought during the past year. Irritation mastered him as his sheepdog, Beth, was playing the fool. She would be with him one moment and the next had vanished and whistle as he would, she did not come.

'What's got into the bitch?' he said irritably. Half the sheep were off the hill and safe in the barn by the farmhouse. Half were still to bring in and the lowering clouds threatened them; enemies that could bring disaster more swiftly than the Hounds of Hades.

The phrase triggered memory, as Joel sat down for a lunch break, with his back against the wall of the ruined cottage that was giving him shelter. His brain seemed like an out-of-control gramophone record these days.

He had looked at the calendar that morning and had knocked it off the wall deliberately, picking it up and putting it face down on the dresser. It was the first anniversary of Annette's death. He had been so busy with winter he had not had time to note the passing days. From Monday come Sunday he was out with the cattle and the sheep breaking the ice on the troughs and carrying food to them.

There was far too much work for one man, but no

one in the village seemed to want to be tied by the seven-day-week needs of animals, or by the primitive working conditions. The other farms were bigger and had begun to modernise.

His work was unending, with both farms, the cattle and the sheep, the mare and the goats, and now he had a flock of chickens. His day began at dawn and ended well after dark, as he left the cleaning indoors until then. He hated untidy surroundings.

There was endless fetching and carrying, and he had no transport. He needed so much water for washing and cooking and cleaning. There was piped water at Craig yr Afon, but there was no outside tap. At least the hose reached from the pipe to the cow byre and the water trough there and the sheep drank from the many streams on the hill.

The sheepdog had gone again. He was ready to start work and she had vanished. He looked round; whistled impatiently.

Then he noticed a figure in the distance, trudging down the hillside; with a bag on his shoulder. The stranger came up to him, offering to help him get the sheep in. Joel looked at the gathering snow clouds and thought of the other chores still to do; he welcomed the help. The man took the bag from his shoulder and poured coffee from a flask, offering it to Joel.

Joel drank. The bitch would return in her own time. Maybe the weather was making her play up. He wasn't as proficient at working a dog as the shepherds. There was so much to learn, and though Beth was biddable, she knew he was no expert. You could never fool a dog.

Heaven knew what she thought she was doing. It wasn't like her. She was so reliable, working beside him almost until she dropped. He had bought her through the hen woman who had appeared, as she always did, when he was at his wits' end, trying to gather in the young ewes.

'My nephew has a trained dog he's selling,' she said. 'A good little bitch. You need a dog.'

Skip had just died, and he missed the animal. The dog had not thrived and maybe had grieved for Annette; maybe Arfon had neglected him so much he couldn't survive. He wasted away, and the vet thought it better to put him out of his misery.

Joel bought the little bitch; a working farm dog, small for her breed, but fast on the hill, and she worked her heart out for him. Gradually she crept into his affections, and she slept in the house, and not in the barn.

A flake of snow drifted out of the sky and he returned to the present and stood and whistled. Beth came racing, and was among the sheep driving them down to him as if aware time was short. The two men herded them and put them in the field and rounded the stragglers, and twice Beth vanished, both times for almost half an hour. By tea-time the sky was black with menace and the drifting flakes were whirling down and their hands and noses were blue with cold and Joel felt like a machine man, wound up by a key, putting one foot in front of another, no thought and not much will left in him. He was aware only of the need to get the beasts to safety before snow masked the hill and surrounded them with silence. He had prepared a big barn for them, when the weather woman said that snow threatened, and lined the walls with bales of hay, piled as high as he could reach.

The weather woman was a cousin of the hen woman. The whole family seemed to have odd ways and odd powers. The postmaster said that the weather woman was just more observant than most;

she studied the sky and the clouds; and knew, from long years alive, just what weather followed each sign.

She knew all the weather rhymes.

'Red sky at night, shepherd's delight.

Red sky in the morning, shepherd's warning.'

They'd had a red sky that morning, all right.

Another favourite of hers was:

'Hog's back and mares' tails

Make tall ships carry small sails.'

Joel learned a lot about the village from the post-master who came visiting often on Sundays now, and happily lugged bales of hay, and helped with milking on Sunday evenings. He'd been farmbred, as a boy, and soon recaptured his old skills. He brought Joel's groceries up for him, knowing how little time the man had.

Joel trudged wearily through the snow-covered grass. The sheep were fey with weather, and he needed the dog. They took down a second batch and came back for a third. It was impossible to hurry, even though the need for speed drove them both. Dark was approaching. The man with him worked in almost total silence, occasionally whistling through his teeth. He was a neatly made man, not so tall as Joel, dark, curly headed, with blue eyes that laughed even though the wind bit into him through clothes too thin.

At last all the sheep were in and this time the bitch had gone for good. Joel whistled. Nothing answered him; no movement in the now changing world; white on the ground and white on the hedges and white on the sheeps' patient woolly backs and white on his head and white on the stranger's cap, below the peak of which his eyes glittered and danced as though he were enjoying every minute.

Joel looked at the gathering dark and the drifting

flakes, and heard on the wind that drove against his face the sound of distant baying.

'The Hounds of Hades.'

Their steps were muffled, no sound on the covered path. The cottage door was ajar. Joel looked at it, puzzled. It should not have been open. It would be very cold indoors. There was a horse to feed and milking to do and water to fetch and they were tired to the bone. And cold.

'What did you say? What are the Hounds of Hades?'

The man's voice startled him. He had not realised he had spoken aloud.

'My grandfather used to say they drove a man to the edge of despair and beyond it to hell unless he had courage to turn and face them and defeat them with his own conviction that life had purpose and meaning.'

'The hounds at the kennels,' the man said, listening. The wind did not often blow from the huntsman's cottage. 'Have you faced your pack?'

The pack lived with him. There was no answer.

'Where is that bitch?' Joel asked irritably, as he opened the cottage door. How did it come to be ajar?

'Come in for a hot drink, and you're welcome to eat, and to warm yourself. It's a wild night.'

He was worried about the bitch. He did not like the thought of her out there in the snow; she might be buried. Suppose she'd gone after rabbits; high on the hills the snow would be drifting.

He lit the oil lamp, and walked through into the big room where the fire glowed, now low, in a wood-burning stove and kept some warmth for them. He stopped, and stared.

'Dear Heaven!'

The bitch was curled on the hearthrug, six pups

suckling from her. It wasn't the first time Beth had opened the door; he never locked up when he went out. No one in the village ever intruded.

'Poor little beast. She came back to give birth to each pup, and leave them in the warm, and between pups came to join us and I never even knew she was in whelp. Where on earth did the dog come from?'

He bent to the pups and the bitch stopped licking at a small blind head and nuzzled the hand that reached to pet her.

'She worked for us all day; and I grumbled,' Joel said. 'She did her job and carried on and made sure the pups were warm and dry and safe. She puts us humans to shame.'

'Life goes on,' the stranger said. He removed his cap, and shook the snow from his jacket, and knelt, hands to the blaze, which Joel had just conjured by throwing on kindling.

The bitch curled round her puppies, and the room was alive with their soft murmuring as they cuddled against her. The two men paused in their eating to watch.

'Have you far to go?' Joel asked, when the dishes were dried and they sat briefly by the fire, one each side of the hearth, the bitch between them, nursing cups of hot strong tea. They needed to get warm before venturing across the fields to the milking shed. No one could take liberties with their health in such weather.

'I owe you an apology. I took advantage of your spare stable. I've a stallion there with a badly cut leg. He was frightened by some idiot that hooted at us, and he bolted, and cleared a barbed wire fence; or nearly did. He caught his leg. The hen woman said you'd not mind giving him a place to rest, and maybe giving me a bed too, and work when I need it. They know me well in the village. My mother was a village woman. I'll come and I'll go, but if you give me horses to work with I'm here for ever. I'm the grandson of a Whisperer; and I've a way with horses. My name is Troy Lee. My father was a wandering man; my mother the village blacksmith's daughter. She died when I was two. My father was a stallion man, and we always lived in stables. I travel with my stallion now, but in weather like this we could do with a place to rest.'

He paused, to look down at the bitch, and then sip his tea.

'No use telling you while you were moithered with the sheep and then the bitch was gone. I hope you don't mind.'

'I'd never turn a horse away,' Joel said. The hen woman knew too much about him, he thought, and put out a hand as the bitch came to him, asking reassurance.

'I've a farmhouse over the fields, Craig yr Afon,' he said. 'I've been meaning to move one day; never got round to it. I'd be better there in this weather, with the beasts across the fields; snow could prevent me from getting to them. I've been lucky this last year, but this looks like a real fall, and no easing yet. You're welcome to stay here, in return for helping, and I'll move there. We can try it for three months; and if it doesn't work out, no hard feelings.'

He needed help, and Troy had worked with him for hours, with the sheep, in appalling weather and laughed at it. You could tell what a man was like at times like this, and Joel felt that he was not being unwise.

Later, sitting milking, Joel wondered if the hen woman had a hand in this too. She seemed to be instrumental in too many parts of his life. Every time

136

she meddled he changed direction, or his direction was changed because of the creatures she sent him.

He'd move in the morning. There was no food at Craig yr Afon. Troy had come with him to milk, taking it for granted that the chores were to be shared. Joel was more than grateful for the help as they walked wearily back through the snow, which now was lying. He went indoors and fed the bitch, and then went out to his mare. She had given him one foal, and another was due later that year.

There was a lamp shining in the spare stable. Joel went inside. Troy was bandaging the leg of a handsome black stallion, who turned his head to look at the intruder, and snorted.

'That'll do,' Troy said. 'Meet Lucifer.'

'Lucifer, son of the morning.' Joel looked at him enviously. He was beautiful; a regal animal, full of his own importance.

'He's gentle,' Troy said. 'We spend so much time together; on the road from farm to farm; or sleeping in barns or stables. He's nearly ten now. He'd give your mare a lovely foal; just right for her. In payment, like.'

Troy was still there when the daffodils bloomed. Joel had moved to the farmhouse across the fields. Troy was an asset, working tirelessly, laughing, and making Joel laugh. They kept one of Beth's dog pups, and when Troy and the stallion took to the road again, the pup was to go with them. He named him Carnon, for no reason at all he said, except he'd never known a dog with such a name and it was different.

They slaved on both farms; piped water to Llain Grin; built more stables, and, several times, Troy brought back a mare with him, one of Lucifer's daughters, when he came home.

'In payment, like,' he said, every time. Joel charged no rent.

Joel forgot the Hounds. Troy kept his devils away from him. By the time they had ten mares at the two farms, Troy had stopped travelling. The mares came to Lucifer.

The letter from Freda arrived one hot summer day, when Troy had been with Joel for three years.

Dear Joel,
The man who bought Sharina has gone bankrupt. He's being prosecuted for neglect. The horses were going to be put down. I rescued Sharina. Do you want her? She'll never breed again. I know how much you loved her; maybe you can give her a few happy months. She's not known any happiness for some years. If you want her, phone me. I'll send Sam with her; I don't suppose you have transport. Torr told me what happened about your inheritance. It was bad luck, but maybe it was for the best. Who knows?

Freda had never been noted for letter writing. She wrote at Christmas; a few brief lines, and that was all.

Joel rang immediately. They had just had the telephone installed. It made it easier to order feed, and deal with the business that was beginning, too slowly, to grow. There was money coming in, but never enough.

Sharina was going to be his, at last. She must now be sixteen years old. The foals he had yearned for from her would never be his.

Freda warned him: the mare looked as if she might die before she even reached him. Did he want to take the risk of the journey? If not, she'd have her put down.

That was unthinkable. He had to try.

He thought of the hen woman. You'll get what you want, but never the way you want it. Far away on the

138

wind, he thought he heard the the kennelled hounds baying. If only his father hadn't sold the farm. If only he hadn't sold Sharina.

If only . . . There was a keening on the wind.

The Hounds of Hades were back, snarling at his heels.

CHAPTER 14

Troy had cooked supper at the cottage, but Joel had eaten little. He checked the lane impatiently, time and again, longing to hear the grind of gears as the vehicle came up the hill. It was almost dusk when the horse-box arrived. Joel knew the driver; a quiet elderly man who drove Freda's horses for her, and had done for years.

'I'm sorry, Sam,' Joel said, 'there's a bit to go yet. I forgot to tell Mrs Harris I've moved to another farm. It's just across the fields, but it's a few miles yet by road; a long way round.'

'I'll go over the footpath and take food,' Troy said. 'You'll be hungry?' he asked Sam.

'I'll be glad of a bite and bed for the night, even if it's in a stable,' the man said. 'It's a weary way from Newmarket, and the roads don't get better.'

'I can make up a bed for you here,' Troy said, knowing there was no spare bed at the farmhouse. Joel, impatient, was already in the passenger seat. They turned, down the narrow lanes, past the church with its Norman tower, past the narrow high Chapel building half a mile further on, along the Straight Mile, and then into the lane and up to Craig yr Afon.

Sharina stood in the box, legs and tail bandaged to protect her, and stared at him. Had it not been for her colour and markings he would never have recognised her. Her coat was dull; her eyes blank; and she was so thin he could see ribs and bones protruding from her body. Her mane and tail were clean and brushed, but the shine had gone.

He could say nothing. He took her halter to lead her down the ramp and out of the box. She followed him slowly, the life half gone from her. Sam was watching him.

'Mrs Harris said you owned her as a lad.'

'Yes,' Joel said. He did not think he would ever see her fit again.

'He's being prosecuted, if it's any comfort,' Sam said, following Joel into the stables.

'Not much,' Joel said. Prosecution might bring punishment to the guilty, but it didn't restore the life.

Sam looked at his face, and walked out of the stable, to meet Troy, who came from the kitchen.

Joel stood and looked at his mare, and the hen woman's words came back to him. 'You'll get what you want but never the way you want it.'

'Oh, Sharina,' he said softly, and put his arms around her neck, as he had when childhood miseries engulfed him. Her ears moved, and she turned to him, and, with a well-remembered gesture, dropped her tongue into his hand.

He was aware of Troy behind him, and the soft startled whistle of shock.

'Dear Heaven,' the man said. 'We've work ahead of us.'

There was little to be done except leave her to rest, and hope she might pull at her haynet. Joel went into the house. Troy had put sandwiches and hot strong tea on the table, and Sam was sitting, eating. He and Troy began to talk quietly.

Joel took a sandwich and walked into the yard. Anger was riding him, so that he longed to go and kill the man who had brought his mare to this sorry state. He had not felt such rage since his father died. He

141

took a bite of the bread, and then flung the rest to Beth, who lay in the light cast from the open kitchen door, nose on paws, forlorn, afraid that the waves of anger were directed at her.

'We'll be off,' Troy said. 'I've cleaned the plates and mugs. Your tea's cold. Anger won't help her, Joel. It's our hard work that will bring her back to health. This is where I start paying my keep; I told you I was a horse wizard. I promise, she'll come right. Not for a long time; but she'll come right.'

Joel heard the sound of the engine die away. He sat on the farmyard wall, listening to the night sounds. The cattle breathing in the field behind him; an owl hooting, and an echoed answer; the sudden yelp of a fox; the strange sound that he now knew was a hedgehog, foraging and calling to its mate; the babble from the running water, and a large animal drinking; the soft whisper of a rising wind rustling the trees. By morning it would be a raging gale, bending the branches, flinging dead wood from the trees and uprooting old stock in the nearby woods.

Mowser mewed, and rubbed around his legs. Beth had crept to her master's feet, and was lying with her nose on his shoe. Polly and Topsy, the two kittens, now more than half-grown, were prowling in the darkness.

There was a half moon, and bright scattered stars, glinting above him. He thought of worlds beyond this, and himself an isolated unimportant speck on a tiny globe in a tiny part of the universe. He was diminished to nothing; the stars and moon had been there, long before he was born, and would be there, long after he was dead.

Annette and he and Arfon would be forgotten. A brief living, a brief suffering, a brief misery. Was that all that life was about? Beth sat up and licked his hand,

and pressed against him, wanting to be remembered, wanting her bed.

Joel went to his, aware that if he didn't he'd never wake for the morning milking.

Lying awake, watching the moon ride across the sky, he felt that whatever gods had watched over his birth had hated him, and that he had been doomed from the start to a life of unhappiness. Cross-starred, his mother had once said of an acquaintance of hers, in his hearing, when he was very small. He had not known what her words meant, and didn't now, but they seemed to fit him.

He woke sour-tempered and weary, as if he had not slept at all, and went down to join Troy in the milking parlour. The familiar chores soothed him, as he washed udders, and sat milking. The Friesians were healthy beasts, and biddable. The little Jersey cow that had been Annette's pet was favoured by both men, and they vied to milk her. Troy had won that game today, and was sitting with her when Joel came down.

The unmilked cattle waited their turn patiently in the yard.

'Sam gone?' Joel asked.

'He had a bite of breakfast and went as soon as he had finished. He told me the story of that mare of yours. Want to hear?'

'Yes,' Joel said.

'The man who bought her had been speculating; tag end of the crash caught him. He didn't want to give up his horses; so he kept too many; not enough money for men; not enough money for food. He began to drink heavily; and the men he had drank too. That was how she lost the foal; they tore it from her. It was big; a colt foal, and wrongly laid. They didn't bother with the vet; he cost money. They killed the foal in delivering it, and damaged her; and still they

143

didn't get the vet. She went septic. That was when one of the lads reported him, and got beaten up for doing so. The vet came, and said she needed a great deal of care and good feeding, and even then she was so badly damaged she could never foal again; that would mean she could never pay for her keep, and so they sent for Mick Muggins, the knacker. Sam said you'll know Mick.'

Joel did know Mick. He was known in every stables and on every farm all round the area, and spoken of with kind laughter as the softest touch in the business. He had inherited the trade from his father, but he wanted to breed horses, not destroy them, and all his profits went in rescuing animals sent to be put down. He'd built a thriving business on his rescue work, founded on a Shire mare, in foal, sold because the farmer went bankrupt. Mick told Freda of Sharina, one day when she went to settle a bill with him. He also sold feedstuffs. She had recognised the mare, and knew that Joel might want her back, even if only to die in his stables, being cared for again, and loved again, as she had been once, long ago.

'Give her some honey,' Troy said. 'About two tablespoons daily; it's the way the Arabs reared their foals; and will give her some energy, and something of a treat as well; she needs something to look forward to; to stimulate her interest in life. There's not much left.'

Joel by now was used to Troy's ideas on horse feeding. He was always impressed when he saw Troy and Lucifer together. Lucifer was never allowed his own way, and he was never punished. He had to do as he was told; Troy used a mixture of coaxing, laughter, and firmness, that always worked. He knew to a fraction of a second just when it was necessary to change his attitude. Lucifer was the best mannered

144

stallion Joel had ever seen.

He remembered Pain only too well.

Pain was liable to rear and kick. Lucifer might want to rear, but at the first signs of such behaviour Troy's voice calmed him.

'What do you think you're doing?' and the stallion stood, and looked at his master, and behaved himself. Brie, Joel's first mare, had had one foal from him. It had been a happy meeting, the mare willing and eager, the stallion besotted with her, gentle with her, courting her.

'It's the way I like it,' Troy said, as he led Lucifer into the stall afterwards. 'It means a happy foal.' Joel laughed at him, but Troy was quite serious, and Joel wondered whether it might be true. Animal ways could be very strange.

They had both looked forward to the birth of the foal. Troy had promised to fit his visits to other farms, with Lucifer, around that date, and keep that month quite free. Joel missed him when he went. They had formed an easy partnership, and there were no problems with mares and the stallion, as the two farms were separated by several fields. Troy had added a Jack donkey to his ménage, and Jaco was in demand among the jennies belonging to the neighbouring children.

Sharina enjoyed her honey. Joel gave it to her twice daily; one tablespoon at a time, so that she began to watch eagerly for him, wanting her treat. She was so thin it would take months to put flesh on her, but at least she was taking an interest in life. She stood with her head over the stable door, watching for Joel and every time he appeared he was greeted by her eager whinny, at first a mockery of what it once had been, but daily growing stronger.

Troy brought dandelions and nettles to mix with her

feed; carrots, which he said gave strong nerves and good blood. He made a tonic for her of hop shoots, marigold flowers and strawberry leaves, and varied her diet with pulped roots, with cooked barley, and told Joel to feed her daily on bran, molasses, and linseed meal. All that was wrong with her now was poor feeding, over a long period, and she had suffered from lack of nourishment when she was carrying the foal, as well as from the resulting infection after such brutal treatment.

Joel was fascinated by many of Troy's treatments, and Rob Thomas, his vet, laughed at them, but was forced to admit that the unorthodox prescriptions for Sharina were having an effect. One of them consisted of garlic roots and fenugreek seed to combat infection.

'I'm not sure she isn't just responding to affection and care and attention,' Rob said one day, after he had been to treat one of the cows for a torn udder. She had decided to jump a barbed-wire fence and go exploring. 'Perhaps our witchdoctor has a recipe to cure Marigold of the wanderlust; or maybe you could butter her hooves the way the hen woman insists her kittens' paws should be buttered, to make them recognise their new homes.'

Troy grinned. He was used to Rob's teasing.

'She'll settle down when she's been to the bull again. No cow's going frisking with a calf inside her; she's too weighty for jumping.'

Within two months Sharina was beginning to resemble her former self; the weight was returning, and she was eager for Joel's company. He began to walk her daily, at first only a few yards, and then gradually increased the distance to a couple of miles round the lanes each day. Maybe when she was fit again he could ride her. He had ridden her, in those long-ago days before she went to the stallion for her

146

first foal. She had raced in her first years, before Grandfather bought her; and won both maiden and novice stakes.

Christmas caught them both unawares. Joel had gone into the post office to buy his paraffin, when old Mr Savage pointed to the calendar. Joel whistled, wondering where the days had gone.

'Your turn to come to me,' he said. 'Sample Troy's cooking. He's a wizard at that as well as with horses.'

It was a meal that was memorable to all of them. Troy cooked duck with orange sauce; tiny crisp game chips; glazed carrots and cabbage that had been cooked for a few seconds only, and then fried, chopped fine, with onions. The Christmas pudding was dark and rich, flaming with brandy sauce, and there were holly wreaths on every outer door, including the stable doors.

They ate at the end of the day, when the cows were milked and the stable work was done. Only a last check at bedtime.

The old man had brought wine with him, but they drank frugally. There was always work to do, and the early milking needed a clear head. Troy and the post-master would have to walk across the fields by the footpath to go home.

Troy had made a table centre of holly; he had found Annette's swagged cloth; and Joel, eating, was reminded too vividly for his peace of mind of that last Christmas Eve meal, in his cottage, and Annette curled on the hearthrug, laughing up at them, saying, 'I want the happiest baby in the whole world. It isn't good for mothers to drink.'

Later, sitting in the firelight, too lazy to bother with lighting the lamps, Troy sang to them. He sang the age-old carols; and that night, after they had both gone, as he went out to the stable, Joel thought of the

147

long-ago story of the Christmas beasts kneeling by Christ's cradle in the manger.

Nanny had told it to him and they had made a crib and put his farm animals round it. He had been very small indeed then. He stood by the mare, stroking her soft neck, looking into her dark eyes. He had her back again; his mare, but the future he had intended to found on her could never be. Rob had confirmed that she could never have another foal.

He closed the stable door, whistled to Beth, who had been off into the dark, and went indoors. The room was filled with the scent of lilac. He had not noticed it for months. He did not feel like sleep. He took the farm accounts and began to work on them, but that was no ploy for Christmas Day. He sat, until the fire was ash and the dog asleep and the moon was about to set, and tried to write a poem.

> I remember a night
> That you filled with delight,
> When you came to my room.
> Now there is only memory.
> I dream of you,
> I yearn for you . . .
> You that were never mine.
> I cannot bear the spring time,
> When lilacs bloom.

He stared at it. He threw the crumpled paper on to the flames, and watched the words die to a small ash that seemed a symbol of his lost hopes.

It was hours before he slept.

PART III   The Hounds of Hades are Silenced

CHAPTER 15

I became more and more intrigued to discover the truth about Great Uncle Joel's secret. Two of my great aunts are still alive: Great Aunt Helene is a daunting lady whom I would not dare to question, but Great Aunt Suzanne is a gentle woman, very sweet natured, and my mother and father have always been extremely fond of her. She is a tiny woman, with prettily waving white hair, and blue eyes, and a gift of laughter.

Great Aunt Diane died when I was only eleven. My grandmother, the fourth sister, Louise, was a formidable lady who none of us regretted very much at her death. We didn't see much of the others, but grandmother visited us, or we visited her, but she was a stern, aloof woman, and never even kissed us. She was always quick to reprimand us, so that we were afraid of her tongue.

There were things I could find out without betraying confidences. Family history is always fascinating, and I am a favourite with Great Aunt Suzanne.

Although she is almost eighty she is very active still in local affairs. Her husband died when their home was bombed during the Second World War. Great Aunt Suzanne must also have thought at times that the Hounds were baying at her heels. She had not had an easy or very happy life. Now she seemed to have come into a quiet anchorage.

Her eldest daughter had married a prosperous solicitor. They had bought a large house, and converted five rooms into a granny flat. They were spacious rooms, kind to Great Aunt Suzanne's furniture, which belonged to an era of enormous side-boards and large dining tables and straight-backed uncomfortable chairs that took up a good deal of room.

I visited her one June afternoon, when the French windows were open to the garden and the sun stood high and blazed down, and the roses were in bloom. The garden table was laid with a lace-edged cloth; spread with the fragile china that she had inherited from her own mother; and there were home-made scones and rock cakes and cucumber sandwiches, and tea in a silver pot.

'I am quite sure there would be less violence if people still had afternoon tea,' she said. 'It's such a civilised meal.'

I laughed, and was promptly rebuked.

'I'm quite serious, Joel dear. Everyone is so busy these days; making money, or striking, or rushing around buying things. We had leisure when I was young; we moved more slowly, had time to sit and think, to be courteous to one another. Shopping was a pleasure. You never knew Mr Munton, did you, dear? His shop smelled of fresh-ground coffee and cheese, and he always had sweeties for us little girls. A toffee for my pretty, he'd say, and we'd discuss the weather and the King and Queen and their children. Nowadays you are lucky if the girl on the supermarket cash desk even looks at you. I don't like modern times at all, Joel.'

It was peaceful in the summer garden. The borders were filled with flowers; the lawns mown; we were back in time to another era, perhaps to the era in which Great Uncle Joel had been a little boy. The garden chairs were far more comfortable than those indoors. I leaned back, and ate cucumber sandwiches, and scones with butter and jam, and a huge slice of fruit cake.

'You are much too thin, dear,' Great Aunt Suzanne said.

'I'd be as fat as butter if I had tea very often with you, Aunt Susie,' I said. Great Aunt Suzanne had always been too much of a mouthful and when we were small she told us to call her Aunt Susie.

'So my brother left you his horses,' she said. 'He chose wisely. You were never suitable for a business life. You are as much of a Viking as old Joel was himself.'

'What was he like as a boy?' I asked.

'He was all boy. That was the trouble. Mother had four dutiful daughters and suddenly she hatched a rebel. Joel always wanted to know; wanted to be doing; he could never sit still; he never walked anywhere; he ran; he was quick-tongued and impatient and wanted everything to happen yesterday.'

She sat, remembering. She was bird-thin herself, with sharp movements that yet had a trained grace.

'He made me laugh. We had to learn deportment, and walk with books on our heads, and he'd see us through the window and walk across the lawn, mincing, as if he had a book on his head. And then Misnid was angry with me, because I wasn't taking my task seriously. She was always angry with poor Joel. Everyone seemed to be angry with him, all the time. He made father furious; he never could do right for mother.'

She sighed.

'You don't want to be bored with all this.'

153

'I do. After all, he left me all he possessed. I want to know all I can about him, everything you can remember.'

'It's strange,' she said. She took a yellow rose from the silver vase in the centre of the table, and held it, as if it would help her to recall the past.

'I was eight years old when he was born. Mother was ill for weeks afterwards; or at least, she seemed to be. He had a nurse, and we rarely saw him. There was school, and we had dancing lessons, and deportment lessons, and the baby was kept upstairs in the attic nursery. We had a play room of our own. It was an odd house, very narrow, but so many rooms. It was an ugly house.'

It was strange to listen to her; her point of view was so very different from her brother's, but he too had thought it an ugly house.

'You don't know how lucky you are, Joel,' she said, after a few minutes' silence in which every bird in the garden seemed to be singing. 'You were allowed to be a child. Your mother encouraged you to ride; you had so much freedom. Our parents were very Victorian, and we had to behave. Our books were all improving books. We had nothing like the books that children can read today. We read Dickens and Thackeray; we spent Sundays learning psalms, going to Sunday school and later, to church three times every Sunday.'

She poured more tea and cut another huge slice of cake.

'I don't often see you,' she said. 'You won't get fat in one afternoon. I made it specially for you; you always loved my cut-and-come-again cake; and my Christmas cake.'

I took the cake, and laughed at her.

'You're a far better cook than my mother,' I said,

and watched the little smile light up her lips and eyes. 'Please go on.'

'You look very like your Uncle Joel did, when he came home on that dreadful day. We were never a happy family. Father disciplined us. Mother saw that we were never idle. We embroidered; we sewed for the poor; we knitted our own jerseys, and father's socks. I still feel guilty if I sit with idle hands. Satan finds work for idle hands to do, mother said, and if she saw us sitting without some piece of work, we had to start on one. We were allowed to make the sweets for her dinner parties; I always was good at trimmings; trifles and mousses, pies and decorated cakes. The cook always did the plain cooking. It was very plain. Boiled beef and dumplings; apple pies; suet puddings.'

She seemed to have forgotten me; to have gone back to a long time ago, so long before I was born. It was a past that was easy to visualise, as I had read so much of Great Uncle Joel's diaries. I hadn't finished them. I had become increasingly fascinated, wanting to build out the story, to know more about him, to see him through his sister's eyes.

'Joel wasn't wicked, though my mother thought he was. It was no life for a boy. It was a very feminine household, and my father, though far from effeminate, was not a really masculine man. Strangely, he went shooting every year on the estate of a lord who was one of the bank's clients. It was most out of character, but I suppose he did it for business reasons, the way so many men play golf for business reasons. He enjoyed reading; and music. He was not interested in any kind of physical game, and Joel was very physical. He was so energetic he made me tired, just watching. He was so full of life. I don't think we took a lot of notice of him. He was ten when I was eighteen;

he was twelve when I married. I think maybe I married to escape from home, and when he ran away I understood so well. Father did a dreadful thing, selling the farm and stud, but he could never understand what he had done. Mother was very bitter; she felt she had been overlooked and that Joel had worked on the old man to get his money. But Joel wasn't like that at all.'

Great Uncle Joel had adored his grandfather. That was plain in everything he wrote. I didn't want to tell his sister about the diaries. I wasn't even sure they were meant for my eyes; perhaps I should have destroyed them, unread, but Great Uncle Joel was dead, and no one else would see them. I would never betray his confidences.

'I loved being married,' Aunt Susie said. 'John came from a big family, and when we went to his home it was like the home I had never had; full of laughter and conversation and nobody minded if you said the wrong thing, or dropped your bread and butter on the floor, or brought mud into the hall on your shoes. I tried to make a home that was a good place to visit, always.' There was a wistful look on her face, and I felt a sudden twinge of guilt. I hadn't visited her since I inherited the stud farm; and now I had only come for information.

'It's a lovely place to visit,' I said. 'And now the farm's running easily I'll come more often. There's been so much to learn.'

'I'd like to see it,' Aunt Susie said, unexpectedly. 'I've often wondered about poor old Joel. It's good to know he got what he wanted in the end. I felt terrible that day, when he came, not knowing. It was a dreadful time, and not only for us. It didn't affect us so much; John and I had been married eight years; your Aunt Marian was five and your Uncle George

156

was nearly seven. We had no money to invest and John had a good job; we were the best off of the four of us in the end, as the others were wealthier. We had nothing to lose. They lost everything. It was harder for them. I envied them sometimes; they had servants and I didn't. We were the poor relations at first.'

She adjusted the lace collar of her blue dress. It reflected back into her eyes, as she looked out over the garden, as if I were no longer there.

'Your grandmother rang me that day. ''Father's shot himself, mother wants us,'' she said. Just like that. She rang off, and I sat there, shaking. George began to cry; I must have looked very odd. Then Marian started crying too. I telephoned John's office; he couldn't make out what I was trying to tell him, and he came home. The children went next door, and we went to mother. Father had gone into his study and put the gun in his mouth ... she found him. None of us knew how to help her.'

I thought of Arfon. Great Uncle Joel had suffered that too, later.

'Then Joel came. Everything seemed unreal; I couldn't believe any of it was happening. How did we tell Joel that everything he had planned on having had gone? Your grandfather took over; he was always good in an emergency. It was a pity he died so young; a heart attack at fifty-three. But he never spared himself.'

People I had never really been interested in before were coming to life. I hadn't known my grandfather at all. He died just before I was born.

'I watched Joel's face. He couldn't believe it; he looked as if the world had ended for him, and we were desperately worried, John and I. John went out to look for him. He never found him. Later, we all decided to send him some money; not very much as now none of us had much, but if we spared fifty pounds each he would have two hundred pounds to help him start again. We dared not tell mother. But we never knew where he had gone. Not until you inherited. We had no news of him for over fifty years. How did he know of you?'

'He had detectives watching me,' I said. 'I found the bills and went to ask the agency what they had been for; the reports were there too. He checked every year, and he knew I was horse crazy. He wrote at the foot of one report, "the boy has my grandfather's genes."'

'Blood will out, John used to say.' Aunt Susie sighed again. 'These old memories are making me sad. Tell me about your horses. How many are there? How many mares? Have you any stallions? Is it a beautiful place?'

I told her about Craig yr Afon; about the big new house built by Great Uncle Joel and the little farmhouse, across the next field, untouched, left as it had been when he inherited it from another man who had killed himself; I told her of Arfon and Annette, but did not tell her all about Annette. Not about the love poems, or the longing or that odd little entry made not so long ago, under the record of a foaling mare. He had named the foal Cynara.

There was just a line or two, of a poem I remembered and couldn't place.

'Surely the kisses of her bright red mouth were sweet, but I was desolate and sick of an old passion ... I have been faithful, after my fashion.'

I drove home, full of Aunt Susie's too ample tea. Down the summer lanes, where briar rose and honeysuckle scented the hedges; my mind full of an active boy, imprisoned by the narrowness of his home; and of his sisters. Aunt Susie had been an

158

unhappy child too. She had loved him, and had missed him. She hadn't said as much to me. She didn't need to. I wished that he had known. It might have eased some of the bitterness. He hated all his family without realising that one of them loved him.

I wanted, more than ever, to get back to those closely written yearbooks. One for each year of the stud, from 1930 to today. I had skipped some years. I had found references to 1929 in future years; sometimes remembering sadly, sometimes angrily.

I had closed the book the night before on a long passage that did not fit into the year in which it was written. It was written some months after Troy had come to live at Llain Grin.

The hen woman is right. I am dogged by the Hounds of Hades. Nothing I want ever comes to pass as I want it. I dream of Annette. Now she is dead she is mine, as she never could be in life. I sleep in her bed; everything I use is hers, and I will never sleep in another place now, as long as I live.

I have my mare; and her foal. A lovely filly foal; and she is in foal again to Lucifer. That should be a beauty, if all goes well. I am afraid to tempt the gods. I envy Troy. He asks so little of life; his stallion, and his light o' loves, that he takes as easily and leaves as easily as the stallion leaves his mares. He was singing yesterday as I came home from market.

A feather of the Lincoln green,
A doublet of the blue,
'Twas all of me you knew, my love,
'Twas all of me you knew.

If only I could live like that, taking each day so casually, devoid of this driving passion for a place like my grandfather's, for owning Sharina again, and for a woman who haunts me nightly, although she has now been dead for almost two years. Am I trying to prove to my dead father that he couldn't cheat me of my birthright? Or am I fulfilling a destiny laid down for me before I was born?

I don't know, and I will never know, for none of us can know why we are on earth, what purpose we serve, and whether there is a God or a malicious deity making mock of us for his own sadistic pleasure.

Why should Annette and her baby both die?

For that matter, what made Arfon leave me his farm? I am beginning to build on his work. The herd is good; the cattle are profitable; the buildings are sound; I can expand this place, and make it into a good well found stud, in years to come. Perhaps I will enjoy success more, because I have had to strive for it. Perhaps God didn't mean me to inherit easily; perhaps my path in life is to be a long one, a path of struggle.

Nothing has ever come easily to me; not since Grandfather died.

I have never known such loneliness. Nobody cares whether I live or die, except perhaps my horses. And, given a good home, they would soon forget me. No one will weep at my grave.

He was twenty-four when he wrote that, a little younger than I am now. I was nearly home now but I turned the car, on an impulse, and went to the churchyard, parking the car in the lane. I stood by his memorial stone and prayed for him; the man who has given me an inheritance, and who never gained his own. He had to work. I have come into it so easily. Life isn't fair, ever. As I stood there, the wind whispering in the yew trees, I felt guilty because I have known so little struggle.

A man came along the path. I hadn't met the vicar before. He glanced at the headstone.

'You are his great nephew?'

I nodded. 'Did you know him?'

'Nobody knew him. He was a silent man, a solitary man, and could be a very stern man. Yet he'd do unexpected things. He gave money every year; a great deal of money, for toys and other comforts for the poor children in this parish. He gave two ponies to the Riding for the Disabled group here. He never came to church. I used to see him with his two dogs, two pointers, always at his heels. They were old and he left instructions that they should die when he died, and not be left to strangers, who might not understand their ways or have sympathy for the foibles of old dogs. Rob Thomas could tell you about him if you asked. He is an old man now, but he will remember those days, long ago, when your great uncle and Troy first came to the village. Your great uncle's dogs and horses adored him. Nobody, except perhaps for the old postmaster, who is long dead, ever really knew him. He was our village mystery man.'

I told him a little about Great Uncle Joel and how he had hoped to inherit a fortune, and found nothing; and, unexpectedly I added, 'I feel guilty about inheriting his fortune now. I don't deserve such luck.'

'Perhaps he thought of you as the son he never had; the son he was building for,' the vicar said. 'God moves in mysterious ways.'

He walked away through the darkness, towards the church.

I stood a little longer, startled by the thought, because I saw, with sudden vividness, that I was a substitute for Annette's son, the baby that had died;

161

the child he never had. He had planned his future round me; had formed his plans round me, from long ago, when I was only a tiny boy. He had watched me grow, from a distance.

I was the fulfilment of his dreams.

I began to understand then why he had left the stud to me; I had to build, as he had built. I had to make the kind of life that was denied him, so that, wherever he was, I might feel certain of his approval and know that I was worthy of his trust.

I wished that I had known him; had spent my years there, as he had spent his with his grandfather. Yet I felt, through his diaries, that I now knew him very well; perhaps better than I would have done had we met and talked. I would never have known his thoughts.

CHAPTER 16

Curiosity was beginning to master me. I went through the old account books, wondering where the money came from. There were two sources of income: one straightforward, shown on the farming books; but the other income, and there were vast sums from it, came – and still comes – through a firm of solicitors; the firm who dealt with the will, and first contacted me. They deal with all my affairs. I did once ask Mr Sargent, a big old man, with a daunting face, a beaked nose and a head of thick grey hair, where the money came from. He merely raised his eyebrows and changed the subject.

It continued, not surprisingly, to mystify me. Had Great Uncle Joel been female I would have suspected an illicit love affair; and perhaps a will made in her favour; but would a woman benefit a man that way?

Nothing unusual showed up for five years. The farm did reasonably well; it made a living. Troy apparently lived rent-free, in return for his help. By 1935 he was a partner, referred to as consultant and helper. The farmhouse where Annette had lived and Llain Grin were now linked by telephone. Great Uncle Joel could ring for Troy in the night, and have him come over.

There were always emergencies.

I now know that too well myself.

The big 'new' house, built later by Great Uncle Joel, is vast compared with the farmhouse. He worked in the new house by day; his offices were there. Big well-appointed rooms, full of filing cabinets. The records were there, straightforward accounts intended for his grooms' eyes. They are nothing like these private diaries, which must have substituted for friends and confidants.

Tara, who works here as a groom, and who somehow reminds me of Troy, from my great uncle's descriptions and from the village descriptions too, tells me that he rarely went anywhere. He had no friends. He spent all his time with his horses, or alone in the farmhouse, night after night, writing, writing, writing. Tara slept in the big house with the other girls who helped. The unmarried men slept at Llain Grin. Tara told me she would wake in the night and look across and see Great Uncle Joel still seated at the little desk, the reading lamp shining on his bearded face, writing, long after midnight.

'Just as I see you, night after night, reading those big books of his,' she said.

'I've too much to learn.'

I had inherited not a farm that got by but an enormous establishment. We are just over the Welsh border, between English Crampton and Welsh Crampton; neither Welsh nor English, which perhaps accounts for the fact that we do so well. We are close to Shropshire; and mares that come to us benefit from the country air. The village is still the old village, the old cottages now modernised, but essentially the same appearance. There is now a new bungalow estate and a big council estate, there are few shops and the only pub is the old place that Great Uncle Joel knew. The farm at Llain Grin has been extended and modernised but the Ty Bach with its plank over the stream is still there, kept as a curiosity, never used. Visitors stare at it, appalled.

164

'It must have been hell in winter,' my cousin Mark said feelingly, visiting one weekend when snow lay thick. He roared with laughter. 'It makes you think, doesn't it?'

I had shown him the big house, the stables and the paddocks; the stallion accommodation. We still keep the stallions at Llain Grin. It is well over threequarters of a mile across the fields from Craig yr Afon. There are three stallions now, all top-notch Thoroughbreds with superb records on the flat. There are good stables; and a good yard. Great Uncle Joel bought all the fields between the two cottages, and now there is a road that links them, and the Land Rovers and horseboxes can drive down it. No need to travel the long way round any more.

This place cost a fortune. There is no clue in the diaries at all, no hint of any unusual prosperity until 1935, four years after Arfon and Annette had died.

He writes, late in January of that year.

I may have a fortune here; I don't know what to do. I will be stealing from the dead. Yet they had no relatives. No one will suffer. No one will ever know. I don't think I can resist the temptation, but if I succumb I know I will suffer from guilt as long as I live.

The credit won't be mine; and I could never acknowledge it. It will need very careful planning. The source of the money can never be revealed to anyone; I will need one very trusted confidant, who will have to handle the money for me; and send it on, from his own account, so that it can't be traced.

I need the money so desperately.

I begin to believe in Fate. Grandfather used to say that when one door closes another opens. That life brings us to many crossroads, and we should follow the signs; that what is to be will be. Everything that happens is meant to happen; to teach us.

Even now, looking back, I can see a trail that leads me here; to this moment. From the day I was born, to a woman who didn't want another child and most certainly didn't want a boy child. So I was sent to Grandfather, who shared with me and passed on to me, his passion for horses; who promised me his farm as inheritance and left it to me; and my father, who sold what should have been mine, and invested the money and lost it; and killed himself.

His was the guilt, and he could never face the future, knowing that.

Is this guilt that haunts our family mine, or his, if I take that path? Did he bring me to this? Did Fate bring me to this, that I might even consider it as a solution? The farm pays, but never enough. I can live, but I can't have the horses I want.

Sharina is mine, but she will never be fit again; never foal again. One of her first filly foals is on the market. I could buy it.

I am sure what I am about to do will make money. But is it honourable?

I had forgotten time, sitting there, brooding over those words, written so long ago, before I was born. Puzzling over them, for what could he have discovered that would bring him money yet might be fraud?

He never threw anything away. I found all Annette's and Arfon's clothes, stored in trunks in the cottage loft. I gave them to the local drama group. There were books too. I kept those. Many of them are poetry books, well worn, well read, well loved.

I went on delving into the acounts. The first really large sum shows almost two years later, at the end of 1936. Nearly £30,000 was paid through his solicitor into his bank account. There were smaller sums from the same source for some months before that. Then the payments escalate; money pours in, and he writes of his tax bill; that takes the money he needs for more mares.

The ringing telephone startled me so much I jumped. I was lost in the past, obsessed by the past, wanting to find out all I could about my benefactor. The more I read of his diaries, the odder the story became, the more intriguing.

I looked at the clock. It was nearly 2 a.m. Her voice was agitated.

'Tara here. The Penstone mare is foaling and everything under the sun is wrong. I've rung for Dan. Can you come?'

It was the first emergency we had had this year. Late January and snow falling, and a bitter cold night outside. It wouldn't be easy for Dan Thomas to get here, but he would try his damnedest. He is a very good vet.

It *would* be the Penstone mare. Joe Penstone was an unpleasant man, to say the least, always grumbling, and nothing done for him was ever right. He expected VIP treatment when he came, which was too often. Tara, as experienced with horses as any groom could ever be, looked after his mares when they came to us. She had been with Uncle Joel for eight years, and before that had worked in her father's stables. She had sold them, almost, but not quite bankrupt, when he died. I knew that from the more recent diaries, which I had read first, wanting to familiarise myself with what went on, now. The distant past had only recently begun to dominate my thoughts.

The mare had given up struggling. She lay, panting heavily, her eyes staring beyond us at a remote world dominated by pain.

'I think it's jammed completely; it's a big foal. Dan said he'd try a Caesarian if I'm right; she's not too exhausted yet. We might save her; and the foal's worth a fortune. Why did it have to be Lalla?'

I looked at the mare; at thousands of pounds of valuable horseflesh. She was insured, but insurance never made up for a life, and she was young; too young to die. She'd had every care and every comfort. The foaling box was luxurious; the room beyond it where the attendant waited was a comfortable small sitting room. An electric fire warmed it; Tara had plugged the percolator in and the room smelled of good hot coffee. There were two armchairs and a desk where notes were made, as Great Uncle Joel had insisted on full statements of every foaling, and I kept the same procedure. It might help in years to come with another mare, another foal. Those old diaries were invaluable in that they were full of horse lore.

I glanced at Tara's notes.

'I called Dan early. I felt if he could operate we might have a live mare and a live foal; not otherwise. Oh, it isn't fair. We've taken such care of her.'

We had had her much longer than usual as Joe's head lad was ill, and he didn't trust his second-in-command at all. He'd trusted us. She was a dainty mare, with a sweet nature and a confiding way of coming to you and pushing her muzzle at you, asking for petting.

'It's just bad luck. No one can blame us,' I said.

'Joe will.' She poured coffee for both of us and pushed the biscuit tin across to me. I took two and ate them, only half aware that I was eating. I kept looking through the window at the mare in the box beyond us.

She was restless and distressed.

I looked at the clock on the wall above the mantlepiece. I'd only been there five minutes, but it seemed like a lifetime. Outside the window the snow was still falling, but as yet it was not lying. Giant white flakes melted as they fell.

'What would my Great Uncle have done?' I asked.

'No more than we are doing; there's nothing we can do. He'd go in and stroke her neck; I did that, but she's beyond noticing now; she's in her own world, and it hurts. We can't help her till Dan comes. He can't get here for at least another twenty minutes, and maybe more than that. The snow might be lying in other places.'

I went in to Lalla. I put a hand on her belly. At least the foal was still alive, I could feel it moving. She was a pretty mare. Her head was dainty; and maybe her framework was too dainty to give birth easily. We had taken her to Manesty, who was a great grandson of Lucifer himself, Troy's foundation stallion.

'Troy died suddenly about four years ago, didn't he? How did he die?' I asked, coming back into the sitting room, and taking another two biscuits. Eating gave me something to do; none of us ever smoked. It was never wise round horses. Great Uncle Joel refused to employ smokers. Fire is an ever-recurring nightmare fear, a fear of terror, and stampeding horses and gutted stables, and death.

'He died of pneumonia,' Tara said. She was looking out of the window, staring into the dark. I could see the reflection of her face; dark curly hair, dark eyes, dark skin, almost gypsyish. No beauty, but it was a very satisfying face to look at. There was strength there; and sense and wisdom. She is a year older than I am.

'He had a most appalling cold, more like flu, but a

169

mare was due to foal and he wouldn't give in. He wouldn't go to bed; he wouldn't see a doctor. They got him to hospital when he collapsed, but it was too late.'

'Did you know him well?' I was listening to the mare, who was shifting uneasily, rustling the straw. I was willing Dan to come, to hurry. Please God, let him be in time. I couldn't bear to lose any mare; most of all, Joe Penstone's mare.

'He was my grandfather,' Tara said.

I stared at her. 'I didn't know he married.'

She laughed.

'The stallion man? He didn't. But he accepted his obligations and my father was one of them. He helped him start up the stables, but there was never enough money. We all have a way with horses. I've several half-cousins, although I don't know many of them as they're scattered around the country. He persuaded Joel to take me on when he came here; Joel didn't like women around the place, but he accepted me, in the end. Troy and I wore him down.'

The Land Rover braked in the yard. It had driven across from Llain Grin. Dan came in, brushing snow off his hair, and went straight to the foaling room. His young assistant, Pete, followed him. They were both tall, but where Dan had thick dark straight hair for ever falling into his eyes, Pete had a blond crew-cut, and looked like a startled chick.

'Tara's right. It means a Caesarian and we've no time to lose. You know the drill, Tara.'

I have never been involved in a Caesarian before. I kept out of the way and watched the team move swiftly into action. Tara always operated the anaesthetic machine in our emergencies. I stood at the window and stared out into the yard. There seemed to be a rapport between Tara and Dan, and I felt a

170

sudden jealousy that made me think hard about my own feelings.

The clock moved so slowly that several times I went close to listen to its tick, convinced it had stopped. I glanced through the window of the foaling room; but could only see backs and bent heads. The mare was hidden.

I poured more coffee; ate another biscuit; walked outside, and stood, snow drifting over me. So had my Great Uncle waited, often, through one crisis after another, through the years; and I must learn patience, as he did.

Then Tara emerged from the foaling box. 'A colt foal and they're both alive,' she said. 'It was a breach and the foal is a very big fellow.'

She refilled the percolator and left the room, returning in a few minutes with a couple of packs of sandwiches.

'I keep them in the freezer and defrost them in the microwave,' she said. 'Worry gives you an appetite. Eat.'

Pete and Dan went to the washroom to clean up, and came to join us.

'Pete will stay so that he's here when she comes out of the anaesthetic,' Dan said. 'I want to get back; Ros is due to have her baby very soon; I'd rather not be out on a call when she comes into labour.'

He was gone, and we listened to the sound of the engine as it faded into the distance. There was no point in going to bed; I would look in on the morning milking. Ron and Ted needed no real supervision, but it might make them happier to know the boss was around at the crack of dawn for once and not always asleep in his bed while they worked.

I sent Tara to bed. She went reluctantly, but I pointed out that one of us needed to be right on the

171

ball tomorrow; one never knew what the day would bring. There was another mare due to foal within a few days. I only hoped she had no surprises for us.

Pete checked the foaling room frequently. The foal was a beauty; he had cleaned the membrane from him and dried him, as his mother wasn't awake to do the job for him. He was well shaped, and well built; too well built for her. That had been the trouble. He had Manesty's colouring; a typical Manesty son.

Manesty is a wonderful animal; regal, gentle, easy to manage. Loman, my stallion manager, is a wizard with horses. He is a small dark man in his late forties, with a ready laugh, and an easy manner, and a soft approach. He worked with Troy for years and must have absorbed his ways.

He had Tara's dark eyes and dark hair, and he moved as Tara did, a lithe stride that always reminded me of a lioness walking. I stared into the fire, finishing off the last sandwich. Surely Loman wasn't another relation? But he well might be.

Perhaps the diaries might answer the question for me, but it would take me a long time to finish reading them. Apart from anything else, Great Uncle Joel's cramped angular writing was difficult to decipher and tiring on the eyes. I could never read much at a time. Instead, after poring over the records of a few days of his life and that of his stud, I turned to those baffling private account books. To sums of money that made me blink. £120,000 in May only a year ago; where on earth did that come from? Not the sale of horses. All the payments are large.

I began to wonder if Great Uncle Joel had been a master crook.

172

CHAPTER 17

There was nothing to do but wait. How did I tell Joe Penstone if his mare died? Insurance would cover the Caesarian; insurance would cover the mare, but she is a good little mare and would make a good mother of foals that could make a mark in racing.

I paced to and fro, looked again and again through the window of the foaling box, and at last the mare began to move. We watched her come back to reality. The foal was away from her, sleeping.

He needed to feed. Tara had milked some of the colostrum off and given it to him, but he would now be hungry again.

As the mare moved, rousing from the anaesthetic, he woke, and tried to stand on legs that didn't know what they were made for. We went in to help him, and then to take him to Lalla. He was her first foal; it had been a traumatic experience for her. How would she react?

Instinct is a wonderful thing. We laid him by her neck; and she reached out her head, even though she wasn't completely back with us. She nosed him, and then tried to lick him, but she was still too exhausted. She laid her head against him, and he snuggled close.

It was at this point that Tara came back, and sent me off to bed, and Liz, Dan's veterinary nurse, drove into the yard to fetch Pete. There was a tricky calving at a farm a few miles away, and Dan didn't want to leave Ros, as she was not feeling very well.

I looked in on the milking, yawning.

The men laughed at me.

'I hear we were lucky last night,' Ted said. That's the thing about a farm like ours; everybody is interested and everybody belongs. Great Uncle Joel had picked his staff well. They are all involved.

'You can say that again,' I said.

I reeled across the yard, so tired I could barely put one leg in front of the other. I seemed to have been up for weeks. It was nearly six o'clock. I dropped on to my bed, too tired to undress. I slept and was haunted by dreams of a dead foal; and woke heavy-eyed and thick-headed, to wash and shave, and go straight over to the foaling block, where I met Tara, who was grinning.

'Go and look', she said.

The mare was standing, licking her foal's back. He had his head raised to her mane, as if investigating it with some surprise. I felt weak at the knees. It could have been my first disaster. I wanted to grab Tara and hug her. I wondered what she would have done if I had.

'All's well that ends well,' Sid said, coming out of the stable next door. He used to be a jockey but grew too heavy; and he's another horse wizard, but his blond hair and blue eyes couldn't have come from Troy. Could they? I found myself looking at all the hands and wondering.

That night I took the stud account books and began to compare them, year by year, with Great Uncle Joel's private notebooks. There was no comparison. There was big money in the stud now; the foals from our own Thoroughbred mares fetched fantastic prices at Newmarket, especially if there were Arabs bidding. The stud fees were very high indeed.

Nominations to Manesty cost owners a fortune.

There had been nothing like that in those early days. Great Uncle Joel couldn't have afforded top mares. There had to be a clue in the diaries.

That night I wrote up the history of Joe Penstone's mare. One day my son might inherit this place, and my diaries and Great Uncle Joel's could be worth a fortune in knowledge; the knowledge of two generations, written down. After I had written it up, I began to browse through his diaries again.

I found an odd little note that meant little to me, but obviously meant so much to him, that I ended up in the research section of the local library a couple of days later.

He wrote: 'One day I want a stallion like Tattersall's Highflyer. Now that's a name to conjure with. I was cheated of Sharina and her colt foals.'

The library revealed that story.

Richard Tattersall was the founder of the bloodstock auctioneering firm that is still a household name today. Highflyer was foaled in 1774. He was never beaten, and stood at stud for a great many years. He sired three Derby winners, and made his owner a fortune. The Tattersalls' home, Highflyer Hall, was built with the money the stallion made.

In the stud accounts for 1935 is the purchase of Sharina's three-year-old filly, already winning races. She was bought with a loan of over five thousand pounds, and that is marked as paid off in late 1936. The interest was astronomical, so he must have borrowed from a loan shark. There is no clue as to where the money came from to pay off the loan. It most certainly didn't come from the stud profits, as they, at the time, were minimal. The farm didn't really begin to make big money until 1948, when they invested in Aqua Vita, a stallion that had made a big mark in racing, and whose sons and daughters bred true to form and went on to make history.

He cost them more than fifty thousand pounds; and no loan. I have the records here beside me, as I write. He earned it back over the years, and as his foals began winning, so his fees increased.

He is buried beside Sharina in the grove of white lilacs. His headstone says: 'Aqua Vita; our pride and glory. May you have mares in your Heaven.'

By then Lucifer too was dead, and had been for some years.

The stallion yard was not built until 1948 either. Up to then there had been, as old photographs show, three stables, none of them of high quality, but now the accounts show that building began in a very big way. The new house was built in 1950; Great Uncle Joel named it Sharina House. The girls lived there and Great Uncle Joel had his farm offices there, but he himself never moved out of the farmhouse. It cost well over ten thousand pounds to build, which was a great deal of money in those days. The place cost me a fortune in death duties. I had to sell two yearlings and our fourth stallion to pay them. The tax bills here are enormous; we can't even pretend we make a loss.

I became more and more obsessed with the mystery. The huge payments continue to flow in, at irregular intervals. Sometimes the cheques were a couple of months apart; at others three or four followed within a few days of one another. There is also a big portfolio of investments, now mostly looked after by Ian, my business manager, and a very competent firm of brokers in Manchester.

I once asked Ian if he knew where the payments came from.

'No,' he said. 'It's not my concern. I do the accounts.'

I went on trying to trace the history of the place.

176

Suppose the money *was* dishonest? What would I do? Was Great Uncle Joel head of a gang of jewel thieves? Or a drug smuggler? Or the brains behind some huge and very crooked outfit? Did he run brothels, or gaming houses, or gambling casinos?

There had to be a clue somewhere. He wrote everything down. It was just a matter of time before I found the answer.

The diaries for 1948 are full of the building plans and their progress. He was very proud of the business he was founding and in July 1948 wrote:

This is far more satisfying than my original inheritance could ever have been. I am achieving, by myself, everything that Grandfather had planned for me, but without his money. I need to leave this to my own family; blood is thicker than water. I will never marry. I hope I find a worthy heir among my nieces' sons. But that is far in the future. There is so much to do. Troy and I have been planning the ideal stallion yard. It's still not easy to find the right materials. The war has left everything in such a mess. Such a waste of five years.

The diaries show that Troy went to war and worked with mules in Italy for part of the time; he came back safely. Great Uncle Joel ran the farm single-handed at first, later with a Polish soldier to help him. The man married a village woman and his sons now have their own smallholding and market garden, just beyond the new estate. We buy all our vegetables from them.

After reading about the detailed planning of it, I looked at the stallion yard with a fresh vision.

There are three boxes; they are built round the sides of a square, and the mares come in past them; there are eight livery stables beyond them, where children from around us house their ponies, at a pittance;

Great Uncle Joel used them to keep the stallions from boredom; the wise heads can watch the comings and goings and they are greeted by everyone who visits. It prevents bad temper, according to Loman, so I continue the custom.

The cottage at Llain Grin was extended; another bedroom was added, a bathroom, and a modern easy-to-run kitchen. A later wing added three more bedrooms, so that all the men could sleep over there. It kept them well apart from the girls.

The big house was used for the girls, with a house-keeper to run it. She died a year ago and since then Tara has coped, but I must get someone else. It's difficult to find the right kind of person. When Great Uncle Joel was alive he used to entertain the mares' owners to dinner there. I take the posh ones to our nearby restaurant, which serves first-class food. Those who are less daunting come to the local pub, where the food is good and the atmosphere friendly. It's easier than laying on food, with all the resulting chores of planning menus, shopping, cooking, laying the table, and then the washing-up. I lived alone in the flat for too long after the divorce not to appreciate the time consumed by the many chores that fall to most women. There is a big dishwasher but it all takes time, and we never have spare time here, although there are so many of us.

Horses are a full-time occupation. We always fuss the foals and pick up their feet and look at them, to get them used to being handled. Life must be very dull for a foal in winter when they are only out in the best weather.

We let the children fuss them too, but titbits are forbidden for all of them, as if titbits become a habit, the person who greets them with no food in his hand may get bitten out of annoyance. It's a very bad habit, and so many people do it, to horses, and zoo animals, and dogs, and even sheep, making them ill, often. Making them pester for food, and spiteful if they don't get it.

It's odd, but I've read so much of Great Uncle Joel's thoughts that I'm beginning to think like him. Maybe that's not such a bad thing. I wish I could solve my mystery. It worries me.

Am I receiving the profits of a crime? If so then the Hounds will hunt me as hard as they did him, and I will never rest easy. I wonder if I could give the money away? But that still doesn't make it honest, and it does help with the stud.

I care about the stud as much as he did. My horses. My stallions; and three of the mares belong to me. Little Sophia, who is a Sharina great-granddaughter, from the line that started here with Sharina's foal; she is gentle and biddable, kind-natured and a devoted mother. Nadia, who Tara has christened The Harpy, is very different; a bombastic animal, who, as a youngster was always in trouble. If she could jump and get out, she did; if she could reach a man with a kick she did; if she could make her foal's life a misery, she did. She hated anyone petting her foals, and would bite them in fury; she wants all the attention. I retired her from breeding, and now sometimes ride her. She isn't an easy mare to ride, either.

The last mare, Sam, short for Samantha, is also mine. I don't know how she will fare when she foals. She is a sleepy animal; she spends more time asleep than awake, and hates exercise, doing everything in her power to resist it; she digs in her hooves, and turns back to the stable, to warmth and rest. I paid a lot of money for her – Tara said too much – and I have a horrible feeling she is going to prove a bad buy, and I am going to learn the hard way that I don't know

179

nearly enough about horses.

By 1950 the money was coming in in even more incredible amounts, and far more frequently. The diaries are fuller, reading, often, almost like a book. Each mare that comes in is lovingly described; and so are the foalings.

I began to flip through the years; sometimes he wrote poetry, and sometimes he quoted from other poets. They are always on the theme of lost loves. I couldn't always place the quotes. One night he wrote:

> *They tolled the one bell only,*
> *Groom there was none to see,*
> *The mourners followed after,*
> *And so to church went she,*
> *And would not wait for me.*

There is always sorrow. Sometimes he alters the wording, as he did with Charlotte Mew's poem, *The Farmer's Bride.*

> *She slept across the fields, there,*
> *With him. My love. I used to stare*
> *When e'er she moved. Oh, my God, the down,*
> *The soft young down of her, the brown,*
> *The brown of her . . . her eyes, her hair, her hair!*

And then he writes after that quotation: 'Why can't I write as they do, why can't I find the words?'

Yet some of his descriptions are almost poetic, especially when he describes the mares and the stallions.

The man who, unbeknown to me, had watched me for so long was named John Arkwright.

I went to see him.

The agency was a flourishing concern in the centre of Market Clayton. I might have known Great Uncle Joel would do everything in the greatest style. I was

180

invited into a carpeted office with a large desk, filing cabinets and bookshelves against two walls, from floor to ceiling, filled not with reference books but with a remarkable collection of detective stories. Hercule Poirot and Father Brown; Lord Peter Wimsey and Lew Archer; Miss Marple and Miss Silver; ancient stories and modern stories, from every kind of author.

John Arkwright saw the direction of my eyes, and grinned.

'When I retire I'm going to outdo all of them,' he said. 'And I will be writing from experience. At the moment I'm doing my homework.'

He tamped tobacco busily into a long-stemmed pipe, and, when he was satisfied, lit it and puffed a cloud of smoke around himself, so that he looked like an impish geni, just coming out of a bottle.

'So you're the heir,' he said. 'Quite a fairy story, isn't it? Pleased with your luck?'

'I'm over the moon,' I said.

'And looking for an heir of your own? More work for us?'

I thought of Tara. I had plans of my own for an heir, and hoped that I wouldn't end as Great Uncle Joel had done, lovelorn and frustrated, grieving and haunted.

I needed to take my time. A slow wooing; getting to know her. I had made one bad mistake with my first marriage, I didn't want another.

'I wanted to find out about my great uncle. I never knew him. What was he like?'

'Formidable. He briefed us; he paid the bills. He queried expenses; he kept an eye on the money all the time. None of us knew him. He came once, in those early days, to see my boss. I was a very young man then, when the quest began. My old man named it the quest; we all thought it rather romantic. The old man died ten years ago, and I took over the agency, but your great uncle insisted I went on personally watching you. He trusted me. I suppose that was something. I watched your uncles for a little while; he soon gave them up in disgust.'

'Why?'

'Nine-to-five men, your uncle called them, no ambition; no sense of adventure. He needed someone to build on what he had made; to take risks, to make his mark, to increase the profits, to keep the name flying. He thought he had found you the day your pony ran away with you. Remember? You went hurtling off across the downs, hanging on like grim death, or however horsemen do hang on. I hate the brutes, and wouldn't get on one's back if my life depended on it. You came off, and good and mad you were. You raced after the animal, found it, and rode it back, bleeding all over, you were.'

'I was ten,' I said. I did remember. The pony was frisky and had been stung by a bee. It must have crawled under the saddle and stung as I came down; I found the dead body and a great lump made by the sting when I unsaddled him. He took off so fast I was nearly unseated. I finally lost the stirrups and pitchforked into a clump of brambles, which was remarkably painful. He ran till he was too tired to run further. Riding him back was easy. It was too far to walk, anyway.

'He was impressed, that time,' John said. He was a big man, with red hair that was turning to grey, and brilliant blue eyes that laughed as he spoke. He seemed to find humanity amusing, which must have taken some doing with his kind of job.

He continued to smoke while he talked, and his left hand constantly stroked his lap in the oddest way, never stopping the movement. There was also the most extraordinary noise. As I stood up to go, and he

182

stood to shake hands, a large Persian cat jumped onto the desk and sat surveying me through slitted green eyes. I had been listening to his purr, under those stroking fingers.

CHAPTER 18

I spent hours every evening that was free poring over those diaries, searching for clues to the source of our extra income. The Hounds of Hades began to hunt me too, so that I lay awake at night, worrying. The extra money helped. There was no denying that, but my inherited Thoroughbred mares produced foals that sold for prices that Great Uncle Joel would have considered astronomical. Horseflesh, in these last few years, especially if it produces winning racehorses, commands the top price in the market.

I too live in the little farmhouse at Craig yr Afon. It has been modernised, but the sitting room is just as Annette knew it; the black beams; the huge grate that takes logs; the inglenook; the enchanting windows, that look out now on to a grove of white lilac that in spring scents the whole farm.

The bedroom too is unaltered. The kitchen has been extended, and is as modern as they come; there is a bathroom beyond it, a huge room, with not only bath, lavatory and bidet but cupboards right along one wall, heated by the hot-water tank. The water is piped from the little fall above the stream, and all three houses have septic tanks. No mains drainage here. Llain Grin is nearer the village, and there are houses close to it now, so it has water from the mains. Sharina House has its water piped from the fall too. That is obviously my Great Uncle's version of Highflyer Hall.

Above the bathroom at Craig yr Afon are two bedrooms, one with its own shower unit and lavatory. I sleep there now. His bedroom, which was Annette's, is untouched. I have left his furniture; his books; all his possessions. There is also a utility room, which houses the deep freeze, the washing machine and an electric drier, and the boiler which provides hot water and central heating. The modernisation has been cleverly done, and, outside, the new building is indistinguishable from the old.

I have brought my own furniture, that blends well with the rooms. I have kept the antique pieces; the dresser that came from Llain Grin among them, with its willow-pattern plates. That Welsh dresser is now also worth a fortune.

Great Uncle Joel had bought Llain Grin and all its contents when his lease ran out. He comments somewhere in his notes, in the 1960s, that Torr died. He had given up racing and was training horses and died after being thrown from his horse while hunting.

We had lost touch with one another. I should have visited him, or written. I owe all this to him. If he had not offered me the use of his cottage, none of this would have happened. At times, when the Hounds haunt me, and I sit alone, by the fire, and remember those early days, I can believe in the Fates spinning. I can believe in a set path from which we can't wander, however hard we try.

And some years later, when he was nearing the end of his life:

I have been reading Annette's poetry books again; there is so much truth in those lines, so many of them, but tonight my eyes found a poem by Masefield. It fits in with my mood.

185

Mine be the dirt and the dross, the dust and the scum of the earth!
Theirs be the music, the colour, the glory, the gold;
Mine be a handful of ashes, a mouthful of mould.

I have known the ashes; have eaten bitter rue; have spent a lifetime dreaming of what might have been. Yet the hen woman spoke the truth. I have all I wanted, yet never come by the way I wanted. My true love has, in the end, been only my passion for my horses, and when I watch them, then I do believe in a God that has some pity.

I closed the diary. Those words were written about six months before he died, when the hand of God, as he called it, was already on him. He had cancer of the lungs, and he knew by the time he wrote that that his time on earth was already limited. He writes more and more about me, speculating about me; whether he is right to trust me; or whether I will fritter away my inheritance and let everything he cared for go to ruin.

One day he wrote: 'God, if you are there, and love me as the clergy say, let him care for my horses as I care.'

I sat, brooding over the past. I do care; I wish I could have known him; have reassured him, but even then, when can a man be believed? So many lie and we never know, until too late, that they spoke falsely.

A few days later I found another entry: 'I would like to meet the boy, face to face. But if he guesses he is to be my heir, if he longs for my departure, so that he can inherit my money, how would I know? It would not be wise. It's best my way. Then he can never hanker for dead men's shoes, as he won't know till I have gone that he is to wear them.'

He ends that entry with a quote from another Masefield poem:

186

What things have the farm ducks seen,
That they cry so ... huddle and cry?
Only the soul that goes,
Eager. Eager. Flying.

So in the end go I, eager, eager, dying, hoping to meet again those I loved in the hereafter. Who would I run to greet first? Annette? Or would it be Sharina?

The hand of God is on me, although the Hounds of Hades hunt me. He calls me. Or is there a devil calling for his ransom; that possible entity men call my soul? I sit and wonder, reviewing the past, the future. What have I done that will be well remembered? What will be ill remembered? Will anyone, in a few years time, remember me at all?

When the days were over, and evening stables ended, and I had looked my last on those wise heads, and patted each one, and smelled the throat-catching smell of the clean horses on clean straw, and stood, revelling in my own three foals, from my own mares, mine to keep or sell, I went back to read the words he wrote during those last months; when he knew his time with his horses was ending.

I felt, as I read, that I had come very close to my great uncle.

He grew more and more nostalgic, quoted poetry more often, made little wry jokes about his pain.

I grow weak as a foal, but have no loving mother to care for me; I have never known a loving mother, and I envy my foals their devoted dams; perhaps I would have been happier as a horse!

Nowadays every morning is a new penance; and the nights are long, and wakeful, and my life's small story reviews itself before me; an endless regretting, all the mistakes I made. I try to remedy them; try to be patient with the grooms, but my tongue grows waspish as the pain devours me. Oh God, let it end soon; I cannot bear much more of this, not even to see my springtime foals this year. Not even to wait for Annette's daffodils; or smell the lilac in bloom; or put yellow roses on Sharina's grave. My chest hurts; I cough and cough and cannot breathe. Dear God, give me freedom from pain; let me sleep, please let me sleep, even if it is now to be forever. I am so tired.

He wrote that four weeks before he died. A week later he wrote:

It will be good to end it, but I cannot take my father's way out. I am not such a coward. It will come, and Death will take my hand, and if I am lucky my end will be as peaceful as Sharina's. She died in her sleep; I found her in the morning and wished I had been there with her at the end, to send her on her way with memories of me, and our long life together; an old mare at the end of her days. She was thirty when she died. Many people felt she was my folly, for what businessman would keep a mare for twenty years that could not even bear a foal? Yet she did bear Neira, before she came back to me, and was grandmother to Cynara; and Cynara, when I raced her, won me another fortune; money comes so easily now; and it doesn't matter to me at all any more.

I wondered suddenly if those first huge sums had come from betting; but they couldn't have; vast sums earned by betting on his horses, the money invested; could that account for the erratic dividends? That at least would be a happier belief than imagining that I

188

was benefiting from the rewards of crime.

Those last months seem to speak of acceptance; almost a longing for death.

Then he wrote nothing for a week, until he quotes again: *'Now hast thou one bare hour to live, And then thou must be damned perpetually! Stand still, you ever-moving spheres of heaven, That time may cease and midnight never come.'*

I read his last words in the quiet hours of the night. Beyond me was darkness and the remote stars and a high-riding moon, and outside only the whisper of wind in the lilac grove he planted.

The last paragraphs he ever wrote say:

I would like to ride into heaven on a charger and meet God on my own terms; holding my head high. Instead I imagine I will be a frail and shivering terrified soul, expecting to be sent to eternal damnation. I think Troy was always happier than I. The stallion man who took life lightly and took love where he found it. Was he sinning? Will I meet him in hell too? I look at Tara daily and remember her grandfather; she walks as he did, laughs as he did, and looks as he did, and has his way with horses and his passion for horses. I hope my great nephew has the sense to keep her on. Tara is the lifeblood of this place. She keeps the lads working; she supervises everything now, and drives them even harder than I did. My horses are safe in her hands.

It is hard to write and hard to think. My strength is ebbing. I went today, leaning like an old man on Tara's arm, feeling the strength of her supporting me, to watch the little black foal born. Everything I do now is accompanied by a voice within me saying 'It is the last time.'

The little black foal will run in his power and

glory when I am only ashes scattered by the breeze. I have asked them to scatter my ashes round Sharina's grave in the lilac grove, and perhaps Tara will remember us both each year with Annette's favourite yellow roses. Oh my God, why must we grow old and frail and die and leave all that we hold dear?

I go to my rest, such as it is, now. I don't know how I managed to get to the stable tonight. I doubt if I will leave my bed again, but when I die I will take with me the memory of that last little foal and my prayers for his future. I love my horses. I cared for them with all the knowledge I had. Surely God will forgive me because of that? My unknown great nephew, if you care enough about my gift of my life's work to you to read these words, cherish your inheritance, and think of me with kindness; I would like one living person to remember me with that.

There is one more page on which he writes: 'The rest is silence.' And then blank pages, as he was only halfway through that book.

I sat, and switched off the light, and watched the flickering flames from the logs burn brightly, then sputter and die. Behind me when I sit in that chair is a very much enlarged photograph of Great Uncle Joel standing beside a mare and foal. It isn't a great picture. Tara took it, when the old man didn't know. She never showed it to him. His eyes are soft with pride as he watches the mare clean her foal. He was so engrossed he never saw the flashlight, and nor did the mare. It was the last foal born while he was alive; the little black foal. I saw him running with the colts when I arrived. He is full of fire and passion, and he runs for the joy of running. I have sent him away to be trained for racing; he was born to race, and he is mine. He belongs to us, the son of one of our mares, not of one of our visiting mares.

I have named him Pejoda. Peter Joel David in short for both of us. I hope you approve, Great Uncle. I hope you are somewhere where you can see us, and know that this stud is thriving, that I have come into a heaven I don't deserve either.

I read and reread everything you wrote. The people you knew spring so vividly to life, though so many are dead. The postmaster and his parrot, and the hen woman, long ago. Torr, who offered you a haven, with neither of you realising where it would lead. Troy, and the many women who loved him. Life is too short. Tonight, after reading your words, written as you were dying, I feel too mortal.

I hoped to find a clue at least as to just how you did make all that money, but in vain.

It needles me, as a recurrent ache does; going away and then returning to worry at my brain. Did you mean to leave me with a mystery, or did you think I would never wonder about those huge sums of money coming from your solicitor?

CHAPTER 19

Tara and I had been married for four years, and our son, Peter Joel, known to everyone as Peter Joe, when he wasn't being cursed up and down the scale as he's a real piece of mischief, was three years old, when John Arkwright came to see me.

He was carrying a black tin box with a padlock on it.

'This is the last errand your great uncle laid on me,' he said. 'Five years after your inheritance I was to investigate your records; find out if you have been running the place wisely. He paid me in advance, and he paid me very well. I'm retired now, but this was to be done by me, and not my successors. I only hope they carry on my business as well as you have carried on yours. You've given him a bonus; a wife he might have chosen himself for you, and a son to carry on the farm when you are dead.'

'If he hasn't been killed by a horse long before then,' I said. Peter Joe seems to think the best place for him always is in the stables with the horses, and he doesn't much mind if it's a mare or a stallion; he gives Loman heart attacks regularly whenever we go to Llain Grin. He moves like quicksilver, and evades our care frequently. The expression of rapture when we put him up on a horse is a joy to see. My son is going to be as crazy about horses as his great great uncle; he can hardly fail, with Tara's genes added to mine.

It was odd talking to John Arkwright and to realise he probably knew more about me than my own parents. He had been a regular visitor to our local pub, and turned the conversation to the stud, saying he wanted a foal one day. He talked to the men when they went there; he talked to the locals; he knew the gossip, and he knew their opinions.

He went racing and talked to the buyers of our foals; and to those who had brought their mares to our stallions.

'I suppose I've been old Joel's proxy,' he said. 'I watched you grow up. I hope you don't resent it. It was my nicest assignment; you were the sort of son I'd have enjoyed having; it's a pity you and old Joel never met. You'd have got on like a house on fire.'

He sighed.

'It's brightened my retirement too. Old horses don't like being put out to grass.'

I looked at him.

'Peter Joe is due to have a sister or a brother in six months' time. Would you like to be godfather?'

'Do you mean that?' There was a brightness in his eyes and the first expression of animation I had ever seen on his face.

'I think I owe you. If your reports had been adverse I'd never have had all this. I never even knew you were there.'

'I was fascinated,' the old man said. 'I watched you develop; and watched this place develop in the last five years. Old Joel chose wisely.'

He lunched with us, and afterwards sat with Peter Joe on his knee and told him a story; a story of a man who watched a small boy like him grow into a man, and have a small son called Peter Joe. We waved goodbye to him and called 'Come again,' and we meant it.

Christmas was over and it was the bleak season before the daffodils flower; but busy for us, because

193

that is when the mares foal and come to the stallions. One of my new mares, little Suzella, was due to have her second foal that night. Her first was a leggy colt, racing in the paddocks when the weather was good. He was one of Manesty's sons; and I intended to have him trained, and if he won well, then he would succeed the old stallion. Manesty is nearly a veteran now. He's done us proud.

When Peter Joe was in bed, Tara went across to the observation room. I do the night stints now; at three months pregnant she needs her rest, but she loves to share the pleasure of watching over the foaling mares.

I put three logs on the fire, and watched the comforting blaze. Peter Joe has a communicating radio by his bed, and can talk to us wherever we are. We are in radio contact with Llain Grin too so that Loman can be summoned instantly if we need extra help. Peter Joe can sometimes be a headache, but he is learning not to babble when we are busy and a 'Not now, son,' stops him. He's a great little kid.

John Arkwright had given me a thick envelope as well as the deedbox.

I opened the envelope, and found inside a letter and key to the padlock. Curiosity mastered me, and I opened the deedbox before I read the letter.

Inside were six morocco-bound books; special editions of six books that, almost fifty years ago had outsold every book written, and with new editions published only recently were still immensely popular. They weren't my type of story, but I remembered them very well; they had been filmed and televised and translated into every language under the sun. A new TV series based on them was in progress.

They all feature the same character.

My mother and sister had loved them. Not least of their attraction was the mystery surrounding the

194

author, Annabelle Leigh. No one knew her real name; she had never been photographed, or interviewed. Some said she was a famous titled lady; some said she was a nun. Rumours abounded.

Neither her publisher nor her agent had ever met her. Some said it was a publicity stunt to help sell the books, but I gathered that they didn't need that to sell. They sold on merit.

I looked at the beautiful bindings; the gold lettering; the gold-edged pages. You don't get books like that these days. I had an idea at last as to the source of the money that came from the solicitors. They were selling off a collection of first editions and these were the last items; an investment, made to keep, perhaps, and only sell in an emergency.

They were in mint condition, and the ordinary hard-backed first editions were worth several thousand pounds each. That first-ever edition of *The Goosegirl* had been very small; they were caught out and had to reprint fast.

Under the six books was a small sealed parcel.

I began to read the letter.

My dear Joel,
If ever you read this you will know I feel I can trust you with my secret, not only with my stud farm. I have taken a gamble, as if John Arkwright died before you had been at Craig yr Afon for five years, this would have remained in the bank safe for ever. I could trust no one else to carry out my wishes.

I think you will have read my diaries, knowing that knowledge was stored there, as well as personal details. I would have read them, were I you, as I read Annette's, three years after her death.

You must have wondered where all the extra

income comes from. I was told it was likely to go on for years. But in time people die, and the men I trusted won't be there, and the truth may come out. I want you to know what happened, so that any discredit is already known to you; I would rather you did not find out the details of my fraud from others. The Hounds have bayed so long for me; I trust they will not bay for you.

I needed money so desperately and life had been so unfair. I found the notebook in Annette's writing desk; and I stole the goosegirl character from her. I hoped she would not mind; I could not give her the credit, as I could not have then used the money; and I didn't know who should benefit. I used her plots, typing night after night, and sent them off. Absurdly, I suppose I am Annabelle Leigh. Certainly the stud is built on money from the sale of her books.

Now, as I draw near to death, it worries me more than it ever did. I could forget at times that Annette was never mine; could daydream and almost imagine she had been my wife and not Arfon's and the dead child was mine. Now, lying awake at night, the coughs tearing my lungs and destroying my body, I hear the Hounds bay louder than ever. When the wind is in the West the Hunt hounds call, and their cries haunt me.

The Hounds of Hades are not driving me to hell; my hell is here, my dying thoughts tormented by the knowledge of my crime against a dead woman. I ask you to give her the credit. The notebooks are there; and you will see that I have stolen her ideas and denied her her fame. I do not know if the world can ever know the truth; do we owe someone else all that money? It is your problem now, and maybe all I have given you is torment of your own and the

Hounds baying at your heels, because the truth would create such complications if it were told. It is now your problem, not mine.

I sat, staring at the letter. I didn't know what to do.

I thought of Great Uncle Joel; the man who had his ashes scattered on his mare's grave. He is beyond feeling guilt, or blame, or censure; but if I tell the world, I will feel the censure.

I sat, staring blankly at the fire, and then opened the parcel. Inside it was a thick hard-backed notebook, and a document that proved to be Arfon's will, leaving the farm and everything in the house and outside it to Great Uncle Joel. The notebook was part of that bequest, wasn't it?

The fear lifted.

I opened the notebook, and stared; there were six titles; and six rough plots. Nothing else. I opened *The Goosegirl* and began to read. I read until Tara came to go to bed; and it was my turn to go to the observation room. I read through the night. The mare was restless but not yet ready to give birth.

I lay on the campbed, but was unable to sleep. I read till dawn broke grey and wet with a wind from the West and the sounds of keening from the Hunt Kennels as the pack was released for morning exercise.

I stared at the book.

It is an incredible book. It is nothing like Annette's plot and, in any case, there is no copyright in plots. It is the story of a peasant girl who tended her geese on the uplands above the King's castle. She was very beautiful, far lovelier than any of the sophisticated ladies of the court. She watched the tournaments, while she watched her geese, looking down on the castle. In particular she watched a knight in silver armour, wearing a blue plume in his helmet. One day, riding, he meets her; they fall in love. He loves her but he is sent away on the King's business. He returns to find she has died and his son is with a wet nurse in the village. The Queen bears a child and because of court politics the child is sent away with the knight, who is also a magician and whose name is Merlin. The royal baby dies, and Merlin substitutes his own son, and brings him up, and in time Arthur is king. A fraudulent king, but a good king. Nobody but Merlin ever knows of the substitution. Merlin spends his life teaching his son, training his son, never telling the boy of his parentage; and also spends his life grieving for the little goosegirl, true to her memory for the rest of his years. The one person in his life who gave him happiness.

I glanced at the other books; the theme was always the same. Loneliness and lost love; and always it is Merlin, wandering through time, in one guise or another, until the present day, when he finds happiness in breeding a stallion that follows at his heels like a dog, and flies through the sky, and takes him to a long-yearned-for heaven, where the goosegirl waits with all the creatures he has loved through centuries of living, during which his life was always shared by faithful animals.

Poor Great Uncle Joel; he had made his own hell. There was no need for it. The words are his; the thoughts are his; the books are his. Reading them, I see over and over again the turn of phrase in those diaries; the stories reveal the loneliness that comes over too in the diaries.

I went back to the house to change places with Tara who returned to the observation room.

I put the books and diaries away. I don't know if it matters now that Great Uncle Joel was really

Annabelle Leigh. The name niggled me, and then I remembered another of his quotations, which again he had altered to suit his own ends:

> All the night tide, I write by the side,
> Of my darling, my darling, my life and my bride,
> In her grave by the sounding sea.
> My beautiful Annabel Lea.

The books are memorials; could any woman ask more?

I had just finished putting the books and diaries away in the chest that had once been Annette's when Tara buzzed me. The foal was on its way. Peter Joe slept in Annette's room; he was awake, listening to us talk.

'Can I come too?'

I picked him up and helped him put on jeans and jersey and his little boots, took his anorak and put it on, and carried him downstairs.

Across the yard and into the foaling block, where the door of the observation room was open and Tara stood, looking down at the foal lying in the straw. A perfect little filly foal; the mare licking her, adoration in her eyes. Tara was lost in enchantment. You never get used to it; it's always incredibly exciting.

Peter Joe ran to the foal before I could stop him and put his arms round it and kissed it, and then stood between us, holding both our hands, his eyes glowing with ecstacy.

'Can we name her Elfwitch?' Peter Joe asked. It was a degree better than his last suggestion which had been Mary Rice Pudding. We had compromised and called that one Marica.

Tara took Peter Joe out and I bathed the mare to wash away the birthstains, and gave her food. She is another gentle trusting animal. Her eyes never left her foal's face. Later, watching it try to stand and helping it to feed, I felt a surge of delight. A live foal. It's never just the money; it's a new being; a new character, to watch develop. This one might race too, might win for me, might breed me great foals.

When the mare was clean and she and the foal were sleeping, I stayed up to watch, and wrote in my own diary.

I wrote first of the foal's birth; and then went on.

'I wonder what the men would say if they knew that their stern old employer had written the most successful romantic novels of the century? Poor Great Uncle Joel; you created your own hell; your unnecessary guilt prevented you finding out the truth. Perhaps you would never have wanted to acknowledge that you wrote under a woman's name, but you could have used the money without being haunted by your own imaginary devils.

You founded the stud farm.

I inherited the stud farm.

Looking at my son tonight, I know that it's his birthright. He inherits from all of us, from you and your grandfather; from me; from Troy, and from Tara. How could he help himself? I must keep it wisely for him, and make up to him for what your father did to you.

Sleep well, Uncle Joel. Sleep quietly, unhaunted by dreams. You did no wrong. You only imagined you did. You left me a double legacy and I'm proud of both.

When spring comes and the lilacs bloom we'll put great sheaves of them on Sharina's grave for you, and take the boughs down to the churchyard to remember Annette and her baby. I have seen their headstone. I'll set a plaque to you as near to it as I can.

Perhaps Tara and I compensate you, somehow, for

200

all you lost. I wonder if you watch us. Who knows?

Your books have given millions of people, all over the world, an hour or two away from life's grim reality, a time to dream.'

The Hounds of Hades are silenced.

I went back to the farmhouse at dawn. Frost on the ground; a grey January day; and as I went into the sitting room, the air was flooded with the scent of lilacs.